EMPATHY ACADEMY

THE EMPATHY ACADEMY

DUSTIN GRINNELL

atmosphere press

Published by Atmosphere Press

Cover design by Kevin Stone

atmospherepress.com

ALSO BY DUSTIN GRINNELL

The Genius Dilemma

Without Limits

Island of Nantucket

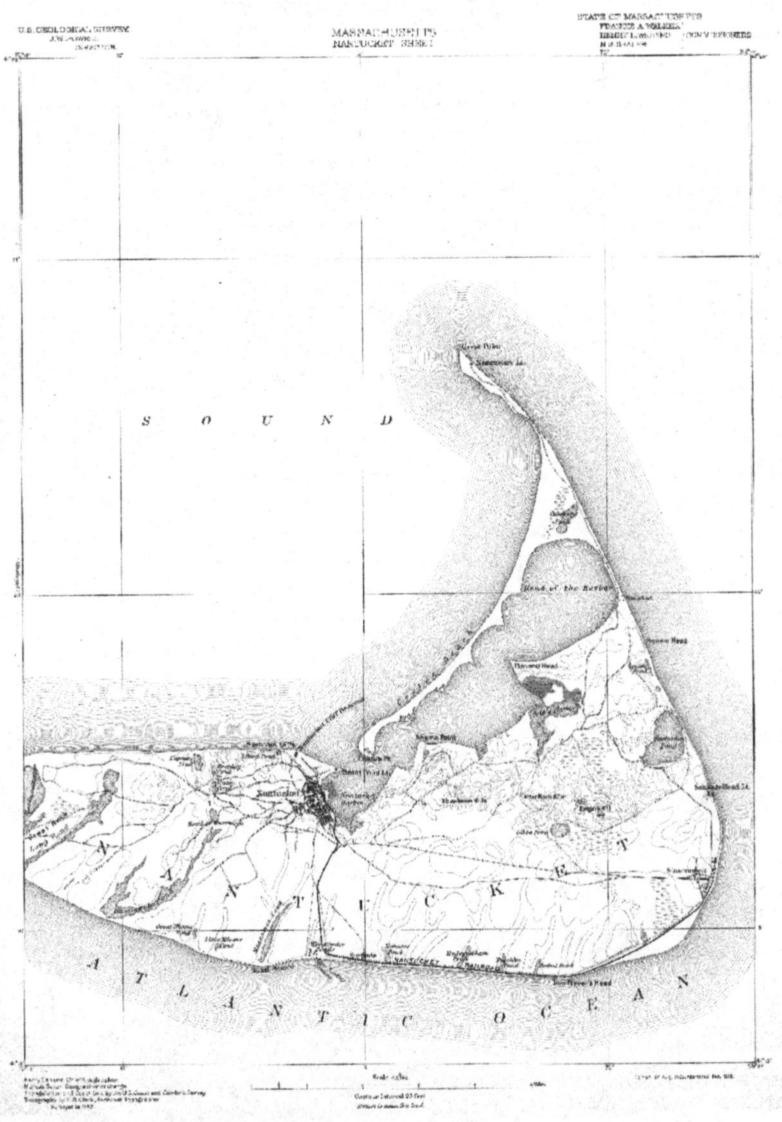

41.28 N, 70.09 W

You can drive the devil out of your garden,
but you will find him again in the garden of your son.

—Johann Heinrich Pestalozzi

CHAPTER ONE

Chestnut Hill, Massachusetts

Montgomery Hughes zipped his duffel bag shut and scanned his bedroom one final time. On his walls hung track medals and academic awards. His bookcase contained a mixture of novels, books on philosophy, and popular science. On his desk was Monty's dog-eared copy of *The Empathy Gene*, the pages inside starting to look like a rainbow from the highlights he'd made during successive readings. The groundbreaking book by Dr. Sonja Woodward examined 'the science of ethics' and offered a prescription for the moral citizen of the 21st century.

Certain that he'd packed everything, Monty pulled a laminated folder from the top drawer of his bureau and walked downstairs and into his father's office. He sat at the desk and looked around the room at the doctor's many accomplishments. There were textbooks he'd authored on cancer. A membership plaque from the National Academy of Sciences. A photo of him with the president of the United States. A framed picture of his father on the cover of *Time* magazine, with the words "Dr. Richard Hughes Finds the Cure" seemingly to justify his smug expression.

Monty set the folder on the desk and opened it to the memo that Richard's lead toxicologist had written to the FDA, blowing the whistle on Avastia. In the public's eyes, Richard had made the greatest discovery in scientific history, but this report proved that his company's cancer cure was a fake. Once the media uncovered that the data propping up the medicine was fraudulent, Monty would be at Woodward Academy on Nantucket Island. He reached for a notepad and wrote, "I know about Avastia." He closed the folder and placed his note on the report's cover.

There was a knock on the front door. Monty jogged through the dining room and opened the door to see his friend Joseph with a smirk on his face. Monty waved him in, led him upstairs to his room, and shut his bedroom door. "Did you bring the letter?"

Joseph pulled an envelope from his pocket and handed it over. "You better pay up, son."

Monty removed a hundred-dollar bill from his wallet and presented it to his friend.

Joseph lifted the money to his nose and sniffed. "The sweet smell of beer money."

Monty opened the envelope and pulled out a letter addressed to Joseph. It congratulated his friend for his acceptance into Woodward Academy.

Dear Mr. Joseph Hayward,

Based on the results of the genetic test administered to you at The Goldman School, you have been enrolled in Woodward Academy for the summer class of 2032. When you arrive, please present the QR code on this letter as your method of identification. We look forward to welcoming you to Nantucket Island.

Sonja Woodward, PhD

Joseph stuffed the bill into his pocket. "How do you plan to bluff your way onto the island?"

"This QR code should get me in," he replied. "I'll use your name at first, but I'll tell them my middle name is Montgomery and that everyone calls me Monty."

"I still don't get why you're going there. Your test was negative, right?"

Monty nodded. If Dr. Woodward's test really worked, Monty didn't have the 'bad genes' like his friend.

"And yet, you're admitting yourself to Woodward anyway?" Joseph continued. "Why? Is this about your dad? You think you're going to turn out like him or something?"

Monty hadn't told Joseph the specifics of his father's fraud. He'd only said a scientist there told him that Richard was involved in something suspicious and the world would soon find out. Even though the genetic test had proven that Monty wasn't predisposed to unethical behavior like Joseph, he still had his father's genes.

"I don't need a genetic test to know that I belong at Woodward," Monty said.

Monty just wanted to be a good person. A good man. But when he discovered his father was a fraud, it caused him to question his own sense of goodness. Monty didn't just get a genetic inheritance from his father; he got an emotional inheritance, too. With a parent like Richard Hughes, was he destined to be bad?

For days, Monty didn't know what to do with what he'd learned. Until he read a news story about a man who'd been struggling to control his anger and was having violent impulses toward people in his life. At night, the man sat in bed and imagined ways to hurt people who'd wronged him. He hadn't done anything violent, only imagined it. Still, he was troubled enough by his impulses that he sought out therapy in an attempt to preemptively control them before they manifested.

The story was a revelation for Monty. It gave him the idea that perhaps he, too, could get control over any genetic or emotional predispositions he might have inherited from his father. It wasn't until Monty heard of Woodward Academy, which claimed to be able to cure adolescents' predisposition to unethical behavior, that Monty knew that's where he needed to go. At Woodward, Monty could rid himself of this terrible curse his father had put upon him.

"Still, sitting in class all summer learning about right versus wrong? Sounds awful, man."

"At least we get to join a sports team and do a community assignment." Monty had never rowed crew and planned to study pre-med when he got to college in the fall, so he'd asked Joseph to select those when Woodward had prompted him.

"Oh yeah, you're all set for crew, and you're enrolled in the physician shadowing program at the Nantucket Cottage Hospital for your community assignment."

"Thanks, Joe."

Joseph sat down at Monty's desk and sighed. "Who knew you could tell so much from a strand of my hair." He snickered. "I've been stealing kids' lunches since the first grade. I didn't need a test to prove I can't feel someone else's pain."

Joseph grabbed *The Empathy Gene* from Monty's desk and examined the picture of the behavioral geneticist, Dr. Woodward, on the cover. Her frizzy blond hair and piercing blue eyes were a striking contrast to the black turtleneck and red lipstick.

"Not taking your Bible?"

"At this point, I know most of it by heart."

Monty had found the book fascinating. It presented research findings from Dr. Woodward's biotechnology company, Moralis Labs, revealing that two to three percent of the population had difficulty with empathy, an automatic process for most people that allows someone to mentally put themselves in the shoes of another individual.

Dr. Woodward's research showed that a person's lack of empathy was linked to a certain amount of unethical behavior, including lying during a negotiation, stealing from an employer, or even minor things, like whether you might cheat in a poker game to increase your chances of winning. According to her research, this predisposition was encoded in specific regions of one's DNA. To identify those who might be vulnerable to unethical behavior, Dr. Woodward created a test that identified genes linked with a lack of empathy. The genes that predisposed someone to unethical conduct had been kept proprietary, but it was rumored that the test identified oxytocin receptors that are involved in empathetic behavior. Clinical trials demonstrated the test could tell how probable an individual was to lean toward unethical decision-making tendencies based on their difficulties with empathy.

While groundbreaking, many were skeptical of Dr. Woodward's research, including Joseph, who often mocked her. The main objection was that a few "empathy genes" couldn't possibly drive complex characteristics like someone's predisposition to unethical behavior. Most people knew that even if you inherit a genetic trait, it doesn't necessarily mean that trait will manifest. For example, if a woman had the BRCA1 gene, it meant she was more likely to get breast cancer, but it wasn't guaranteed. Many people without the gene will still develop cancer.

In her book, Dr. Woodward was clear that behavior resulted from a complex dance between one's genes and one's environment, or nature versus nurture, and that the test just reveals one's tendencies, not destiny. That's why she built Woodward Academy—to address the 'nurture' side of the equation since scientists couldn't yet tinker with our genes to lower one's risk of being unethical. "Yet," being the operative word, Joseph liked to inform Monty.

Joseph shook his head while looking at the book's cover. "What if Dr. Woodward isn't the savior everyone's making her out to be? What will she do if her ethics intervention program doesn't work? Scientists like Woodward can't help themselves, Monty. I bet you the hundred bucks in my pocket that Moralis Labs is already messing with people's genes."

After reading her book several times and watching Dr. Woodward in TV interviews, Monty sensed that the scientist's intentions were good, but he'd taken enough history classes to understand that even the best intentions could lead to terrible consequences. "If it makes you feel any better, Joe, if I see something, I'll say something."

"I still can't believe that our school bought into this social experiment."

Understanding the implications of this predisposition in adolescents, five elite high schools in Massachusetts, including Phillips Academy, Buckingham Browne & Nichols, and The Goldman School, where Monty and Joseph had just graduated, agreed to pilot the test. Those who scored positive earned a ticket to Woodward. When Monty learned about his father's actions, he asked Joseph if he could use his results, to which Joseph happily obliged.

Still, many were skeptical the Woodward program could turn a few dozen bad apples into Boy Scouts. Many in the media dismissed the Academy as an over-hyped psych study: It would give a test at the beginning to get a baseline, instruct for a couple of months, then conclude with another test to determine if changes occurred. Dr. Woodward hadn't revealed her curriculum, a decision that fueled the controversy.

To ensure positive change in the students, Dr. Woodward had recruited professors in ethics, behavioral science, psychology, theology, and philosophy from elite institutions around the world. The idea was to improve students' characters before they went on to pursue careers in the arts, sciences, business, and public services. Many questioned whether these kids could indeed be "cured" of their tendency? *Cure* was too grandiose a word, Dr. Woodward told those who inquired. In her mind, an improved grounding in ethical norms would make youths better citizens and help ensure a healthier, safer society.

Monty checked his watch. The ferry to Nantucket was scheduled to leave Hyannis in two hours. "I have to catch an Uber to get down to the Cape."

Monty led Joseph downstairs, opened the front door, and thanked him.

"I should be thanking you—you got me off the hook," Joseph admitted. "While you're reading Aristotle all summer, I'll be waterskiing at my family's lake house in New Hampshire."

"Do me a favor? My parents will call everyone when they can't find me. Can you buy me some time by telling your parents I'm with you at the lake house for a few weeks?"

"I'd be more than happy." Joseph raised an eyebrow. "For another hundred dollars." There was a pause, and then Joseph chuckled. "Just kidding, bro, I'll cover for you. These bad genes aren't going to express themselves, you know."

"Thanks, Joe," Monty said with a grin.

Monty shut the door and ordered an Uber to Hyannis. An hour and a half later, he rolled his bag onto the ferry and made his way to the bow. The vessel's engine whirred as it pulled away from shore. Monty stared into the misty gray ocean, the breeze parting his dark brown hair. He watched seagulls swoop and bank against the wind.

Several miles off the coast, a giant tail of a humpback whale breached the water's surface. A few teenagers, who Monty guessed were also on their way to Woodward, hurried to the railing to watch the whale spray water from its blowhole. As the whale began its deep dive back into the dark Atlantic Ocean, Monty began to second-guess his choice to fake his way into the Academy. Could Woodward really teach kids right from wrong? Could classroom instruction, in fact, prevent someone from future misconduct?

Monty felt a chill as Nantucket appeared on the horizon. A light rain had begun to fall, and gray clouds hung over rolling sand dunes. The grounds of Woodward Academy came into view. The campus looked like an artist's colony, a smattering of wooden buildings hugging the idyllic coastline. Monty felt a sense of dread as Moralis Labs appeared to the side of Woodward. It wasn't clear whether Woodward and Moralis collaborated in any way. What happened inside the massive gray, windowless building had been shrouded in mystery.

As the ferry chugged toward the sea-swept island, Monty wondered what Dr. Woodward would do if her social experiment didn't live up to everyone's expectations. Had Moralis already started tinkering with people's genes? Did biology or the environment determine who he was? Could he control his destiny, or was he fated to become the man his father had become?

CHAPTER TWO

Cambridge, Massachusetts

Kendall Square was a hub of scientific innovation and home to more biopharmaceutical companies per square mile than anywhere else on the planet. Through the massive glass panels of Nautilus Therapeutics, pedestrians could see a lobby displaying genome sequencers and multiscreen computers playing animations of spinning DNA double helixes.

Currently, the auditorium of Nautilus was full of world-renowned biologists, physicians, venture capitalists, and members of the press. Even the director of the National Cancer Institute was in attendance. They had come to learn more about the new FDA-approved cancer therapy developed by Richard Hughes, a respected authority on cancer biology.

Richard was backstage, still reviewing his speech, when one of his postdoctoral students began to read his illustrious biography at the podium. His phone buzzed in his pocket. He pulled it out to see that it was the hospital calling. He didn't pick up.

Richard texted his wife, Elizabeth. *Monty home yet?*

Not yet, Elizabeth wrote back. *Haven't seen him all day.*

Still on for a family meeting tonight after the Red Sox game?

Of course. She inserted a smiley-face emoji. *What is it about?*

Richard winced. He grabbed his side as pain made itself known.

I'll explain everything tonight.

The postdoc wrapped up his introduction then. "Without further ado, I want to welcome to the stage the eminent Dr. Richard Hughes!"

Applause greeted Richard as he ambled across the stage and stood proudly at the podium. He scanned the crowd, gathering all eyes. He could be theatrical, if the situation called for it. The best scientists, after all, weren't just experts in their respective fields. They were proficient communicators who could translate their work to the public—even perform it for audiences.

"Twenty-two months..." Richard paused. "That is the average time many of today's cancer drugs add to a patient's life. And despite the heralded success of some targeted medications, we don't have effective drugs for the most prevalent cancers."

Using a remote control, Richard advanced a slide presentation on a monitor beside him to show a photo of a shirtless middle-aged man. His torso was covered in bruises and lesions.

"Two years ago, this patient's body was riddled with

tumors. When Peter visited me at Brigham and Women's Hospital, he had been diagnosed with late-stage metastatic melanoma. We started treating him with conventional cancer therapies that targeted his specific cancer."

Richard advanced the presentation to another photograph of his patient. In this one, Peter's skin was a vibrant pink, with no sign of discolorations and tumors. "After six months on targeted therapies, Peter was in remission. He walked out of the hospital and returned to work as a welder."

Richard took a deep breath and moved to a third picture of Peter. Like the first picture, his torso was covered in tumors. "This picture was taken six months later. As you can see, the cancer returned, everywhere."

Richard sipped from a bottled water and let the information sink in for the audience.

"While targeted therapies are remarkable in their ability to shut down key mutations in cancer, the cancerous cells eventually develop resistance to the drugs. One hundred percent of patients relapse."

Richard slowly scanned the faces of the crowd. "Why don't these cancer treatments work? Answer: Because we still don't understand the basic biological mechanisms that drive the cancer process."

Richard advanced the presentation to an animation of molecules stacking on top of the double-helix structure of DNA. "The molecules here are called super-enhancers. They assemble on DNA and act as on-off switches for genes. They control healthy gene function and normal processes, such as cell growth. But cancer cells can assemble their own super-enhancers on DNA to turn on cancer-causing genes. Our research has found that these cancer super-enhancers are extremely sensitive to disruption. In fact, they're a house of cards. Nautilus Therapeutics has spent the last eight years figuring out how to disrupt them."

The presentation switched to an image of a molecule with chemical bonds linking atoms; *Cancer Super-Enhancers* was written below it. Arrows pointed to deep pockets in various places.

"Each arrow points to an area where a synthetic molecule could fit. These are 'druggable' areas; a small artificial molecule could target them. Our lab has discovered forty-five druggable components on cancer super-enhancers."

The next slide of the presentation displayed an image of a vial. "We just received FDA approval for a compound that virtually annihilates cancer. It's called GQ6, commonly referred to as Avastia. When administered, Avastia keeps these genetic regulators from assembling on DNA, thereby disrupting cancer cells' ability to grow."

The presentation then showed Peter, with the words *Two Years Later* running along the bottom of the image. The man's chest was free of tumors.

"Here's Peter after treatment with our breakthrough targeted therapy, Avastia."

The audience erupted in chatter, and Richard used the moment to spin away from the podium and cough into his hand.

When he and the audience had both calmed, Richard turned back and continued. "I'm a scientist, not a businessman." He took a deep breath. "Now that Avastia is on the market, Nautilus needs someone who knows how to run the business end of a biotech company. Which is why, as of today, I am stepping down as CEO. I intend to spend more time with my family and continue contributing to Nautilus as a scientific adviser. Thank you all for coming."

Richard stepped off the stage and made his way toward the exit.

Amy Baker, a reporter for the *Boston Globe*, appeared beside him with a tape recorder in her hand. "Dr. Hughes, if I may–"

"No questions, please." Richard waved his hand and walked faster.

"Is there another reason you're stepping down?"

Richard tugged at his shirtsleeve to cover the hospital bracelet on his wrist. "I have somewhere to be, Ms. Baker."

Amy was adamant, though. "There's been mounting scrutiny concerning Avastia's effectiveness. I'm sure you're aware that no other lab has been able to replicate the results of your experiments?"

"Cancer is a profoundly complicated–"

Amy stepped in front of Richard, forcing him to stop. "Nautilus has been a black box ever since its founding. Wall Street analysts believe the secrecy has left the company in flux, and you've done little to reassure the public."

Richard clutched at his side in pain. When Amy examined the scientist with a worried look, he straightened. He pointed at Amy. "Avastia was approved by the FDA based on extensive laboratory and clinical studies. Now, if you will excuse me."

"What are you afraid of, Dr. Hughes?" Amy asked, stepping aside.

Richard rushed through the exit and slammed the door in Amy's face.

CHAPTER THREE

Nantucket Island, Woodward Academy

The ferry tapped the wooden dock with a thud. A crew of muscular men in white, tight-fitting polo shirts anchored the boat to the dock, tying thick ropes around metal cleats. The students bunched up near the front of the boat, waiting to step onto Nantucket Island.

A man lowered a wooden bridge, creating a walkway for the students.

"My name is Greg Aldrich." Holding a clipboard, Mr. Aldrich was broad-shouldered and had a rough and ready face. "I'm head of security at Woodward. I need to check attendance, so please make a single-file line and make sure the QR code on your letter is visible."

"Edwin Thompson," said the first young man with an air of superiority. Edwin wore a salmon-colored Oxford button-down shirt. Once on the dock, he began taking practice golf swings, as if he were hitting balls into the ocean.

The dozen or so students told Mr. Aldrich their names one by one as they left the boat and stepped onto the dock. The teenagers were quintessential examples of New England upper crust. Impeccably dressed in classic polo shirts and boat shoes, tortoiseshell sunglasses, pearl earrings, and polished accessories. Privileged, with an air of old money. Aristocrats.

Jonathan Davenport, a handsome black teenager in blue jeans and a gray T-shirt, soon joined Edwin, who leaned toward Jonathan and whispered, "Pahk the cah in Hahvahd Yahd," playfully mocking the boy's thick South Boston accent. They both laughed. From where he stood, Monty overheard Jonathan say that he'd made over $40,000 trading in the options market that spring. He'd planned to spend the summer in a cabin he'd rented at Lake Placid in Upstate New York before he tested positive on Dr. Woodward's genetic test and his parents forced him to attend Woodward.

Monty was the last in line.

"Name?" Mr. Aldrich asked, staring at his clipboard.

"Joseph Montgomery Hayward," Monty lied. "People just call me Monty."

Mr. Aldrich raised his eyebrows, staring at Monty for a moment. Then he looked down and scribbled on his clipboard. "Letter?"

Monty held out Joseph's letter and faked a smile.

Mr. Aldrich used a device to scan the QR code and a light turned green. He pointed to a building made of tan-colored bricks with narrow windows and a light-green roof.

"Head to the main building. Dr. Woodward is waiting for you there."

Mr. Aldrich nodded to his security team, and two guards followed the students as they left the docks and strolled down the cobblestone pathway toward the main building. Each guard wore a communication device in his ear, and they monitored the students with sideways glances.

Several of the students chatted as they took in their home for the summer. Near the middle of the pack, Taylor Covington barely raised her eyes from her smartphone, though her steps never faltered. She had spent most of the ferry ride playing games and was clearly still engrossed. Beside her, Cory Maddox ran a hand over his wide chin and shook his protein drink before taking a swig. Kirsten May kept her head down, hiding behind the raised hood of her black sweatshirt and clutching a notebook to her chest. Monty had seen her sketching in that notebook throughout the ferry ride, and he briefly wondered what, or who, had been her model.

Halfway down the path, a sailboat tied to a dock caught Monty's eye.

On board, a man appeared to be struggling to stand up the mast. Waiting until the two guards turned their backs, Monty jogged toward the boat to investigate. As he approached, he was reminded of summer vacations during which his father had taught him to sail on the other side of Nantucket. This sailboat, *Know Thyself*, looked to be about 35 feet long. The person he'd spotted earlier, a strapping, wiry man with black curly hair, circled the mast, holding a rope tightly.

"Beginning of the season?" Monty called from the dock.

The man laughed. "Beginning of *repairs*. It could be

the middle of the summer before this baby's seaworthy." He put his hands on his waist. "Have to get the mast up before she goes anywhere."

Monty had seen a lot of boats, and this one looked old. It needed a paint job and a tune-up, but there was an undeniable charm to it.

"You're trying to do a two-person lift with one person," Monty said.

"Are you offering a second hand?" the man asked.

Monty nodded. "Happy to help."

"Hop on." The man waved Monty onto the boat, then shook hands with him. "My name's Palmer."

"Monty."

Palmer pointed to the bottom of the mast, which rested near a hole in the deck. Monty stepped over some coiled rope, stood over the mast, and awaited orders.

Palmer opened a stepladder beside the hole. "I'm going to climb this stepladder and raise the mast while you guide it into that hole."

Monty agreed, even though the system looked unstable.

Palmer stepped gingerly up the stepladder while holding the mast at his side. Monty held his end of the mast while he watched Palmer carry his end upward. When Palmer was about six feet up, the mast slipped from his hands, but he caught it with surprising quickness, nearly falling off the ladder.

"Are you all right?" Monty asked.

Palmer huffed. "Close call. Let's try again."

This time, Monty lifted the mast with more force until the bottom dropped into the hole. Palmer pushed the mast upright, and the two made sure it was standing securely.

Palmer dried his hands with a towel and took a swig from a bottled beer.

Monty examined the boat. There were diplomas on the wall of the dining area. An undergraduate degree from Harvard in anthropology, a master's in philosophy from Oxford, and a medical degree from Stanford. A framed newspaper clipping showed Palmer as editor in chief of the *International Philosophical Quarterly*.

"Do you live here?" Monty asked.

"Welcome to my floating home. Always wanted to live aboard. I sailed in graduate school but gave it up when life got too busy. At the end of the summer, I want to sail her back to Boston Harbor and dock in the Boston Waterboat Marina."

Monty's father had taught him how to sail on carbon-fiber dinghies on the Charles River, a few hundred feet from MIT in Cambridge. He rubbed the scar on his finger that a rope had given him on the day of his father's first sailing lesson. Monty had owned several small sailboats, so he knew the annoyances involved. "Lots of headaches with these boats. Storms, gas tank leaks, electrical issues, engine troubles."

Palmer nodded. He looked out at the Atlantic Ocean. The sun was beginning to set. "But then a pod of dolphins swims up alongside your boat, and it's all worth it."

He took another sip from his beer. Grabbing a brown leather jacket off the boat's railing, he hopped onto the dock.

Monty followed him onto a coastal path. "Where are you going?"

Palmer tilted his head toward an observatory at the top of a hill. "I go to the observatory to relax. Look at the moon, the stars; get perspective. I'll take you as a class."

"You're a teacher here?"

Palmer nodded. "I like to think of myself as a guide."

"What kind of guide?"

Palmer looked out over a field of sea-swept grass. The tide rose high enough that waves crashed over the grass. "Your future is a bit like a field. I can help you find a pathway through it." He turned and continued up the trail. "Did you know that the word 'education' comes from the Latin 'educare,' which means 'to bring out.'"

"To bring out what?"

"My role as a teacher is to help you discover your own unique talents and bring them out. To awaken you, so to speak."

"Awaken in what way?"

Palmer stopped. "Awaken you to who you are." He looked at the main building. "It was nice meeting you, Monty. Join the others. You won't want to miss Dr. Woodward's speech."

CHAPTER FOUR

Richard steered his dark-blue Range Rover past the neighborhood's front gate. He parked in the circular driveway outside a Tudor-style mansion that overlooked a small koi pond.

His wife, Elizabeth, knelt in the garden, poking the soil with a spade. When Richard's truck stopped in the driveway, she lifted her head over the tall flowers and waved. Getting out and walking to the edge of the garden, Richard asked if Elizabeth had put out a jacket and shirt for the Red Sox game. She said she had.

Elizabeth had always played the part of the "good wife" well. After 30 years of marriage, she was still devoted to Richard. She had stayed at home while her ambitious friends negotiated the rat race. With her MBA from Stanford, she could have directed a mid-sized company or a nonprofit, but she had sacrificed that life for the family, for Monty. For Richard.

Richard gave Elizabeth a peck on the cheek. "Where's Monty?"

"Still not home."

"He's coming with us to the Red Sox game, right?"

"You know how he feels about those fundraisers."

"It's *not* a fundraiser; it's a baseball game." Richard grinned. "With a few venture capitalists from the coasts."

Elizabeth glanced at him from the corner of her eye. "Come on."

Once inside, Elizabeth hung up Richard's jacket and went to the kitchen to begin putting away clean dishes.

Richard took off his shoes and sat at the kitchen table. "You seem tense."

Elizabeth placed a plate on top of another too hard, chipping it. "Too much sun." She looked at Richard's shrunken waist. "Have you been losing weight, Richard?"

Richard cleared his throat and indicated the stationary bike in the living room. "Been exercising more lately." He got up, tugged up the drooping waistband of his pants, and walked into the living room. The television was on, set to CNN. The bottom of the screen displayed the words *Is America in cultural decline?* When Richard saw Ms. Baker representing *The Boston Globe* as one of the analysts, he thought, *Does that woman sleep?*

Amy spoke with authority, with passion. "The definition of 'good business' is that the business is as good as its word."

"One might say that shareholders expect businesses to make money, not set an example," the news anchor replied.

"I'm not saying that companies have to stop animal testing, but they do need to start paying their employees reasonable wages, and they most definitely need to stop stealing from people." Amy moved her hands as she spoke.

"The economic cost of white-collar crime far exceeds conventional crime. Each year, the IRS is cheated out of fifteen percent of its tax revenue. Insurance fraud is estimated to cost more than forty billion dollars per year."

"Business schools are upgrading their curricula with ethics and social responsibility courses," the anchor responded.

"Yes, but you can ace an ethics course in business school and still fall victim to organizational or psychological pressures. Even good, well-intentioned people can fall prey to bad behavior inside complex workplaces."

"Do you think teaching morality is a school's responsibility?"

Amy shook her head. "Parents should be teaching values, not educators."

"You've spoken out against Woodward Academy, but couldn't Dr. Woodward's school teach young adults the difference between right and wrong, if parents fail in that respect?"

"We don't know. Maybe the school will work as insurance, as Dr. Woodward bills it. But she is making a lot of promises, and there are a lot of taxpayer dollars on the line."

Richard flipped the channel to a Red Sox pregame show. The family's Siamese cat, *Gene*, circled his feet, pressing its head into his legs. Richard bent to pet the cat and yelled into the kitchen, "I'm going into the study for a bit."

The study was filled with books and contemporary art. Sitting down at his desk, Richard used scissors to cut away the hospital bracelet on his wrist. He placed the bracelet in the drawer next to yesterday's blood test, which showed a dangerously low white-blood-cell count.

As he closed the drawer, Richard noticed a piece of paper on top of a folder on his desk that he hadn't noticed earlier. Picking it up, he recognized his son's handwriting.

I know about Avastia.

Richard instantly recognized the folder beneath the note. It was the report that his lead toxicologist, Dr. Collins, had given him last month that showed Avastia didn't work—and was harmful, in fact. The same report that Richard had ordered Dr. Collins to bury, but was now, mysteriously, sitting on his desk for anyone to see.

Richard and Elizabeth were quiet for most of the drive to Fenway Park. Richard merged the Range Rover onto a jam-packed Storrow Drive. A man leaned out his window and screamed, "Asshole!"

Richard darted into the fast lane, shaking his head. "Boston drivers are the worst."

In the passenger seat, Elizabeth's hands were clasped tightly in her lap. Her eyes flitted over the joggers and cyclists hugging the Charles River.

"Why didn't you tell me you were going to resign, Richard?"

The truck entered Kenmore Square. Mobs of people were crossing the streets on their way to Fenway Park.

"I wonder who the starting pitcher is tonight."

"If you're not running Nautilus," Elizabeth said, "what are you going to do?"

Richard turned to look at her. "I'll take an early

retirement. I can spend more time at home, maybe dabble in photography." He smiled. "Remember when I won that photography contest?" He placed his hand on Elizabeth's knee. "I want to spend time with Monty this summer before he goes to Harvard in the fall."

Elizabeth avoided her husband's gaze. Through the window, she watched the sun disappear behind the ballpark. Her eyes were damp with tears.

In the passenger seat of a black suburban, FBI agent David Holiday ran a hand through his scruffy beard. *How will Dr. Hughes react when I flash an arrest warrant in his smug face?*

Holiday led an arm of the FBI that focused on white-collar crime. Through experience, he'd seen the devastating effects of financial scams that, for some people, could be worse than death. But Dr. Hughes had reached a wicked kind of low for a white-collar criminal. He was getting rich, and enormously famous, off a cancer drug that did nothing.

A dozen members of Holiday's fraud unit, accompanied by officials from the IRS, barreled through the lobby of Nautilus Therapeutics. The uniformed team fanned out across the building, demanding that employees stop working and leave their workstations. They riffled through filing cabinets and stuffed boxes with papers and hard drives.

Meanwhile, Holiday's suburban screeched to a halt in front of Fenway Park. He flashed his badge and marched past security. He climbed the stairs to the box seat section of the park.

From the balcony of his box seat, Richard felt a crisp breeze on his face as he watched the pitcher hurl a baseball toward home plate. Behind Richard were some of Boston's elite, including the Massachusetts governor, leaders of nonprofits, entrepreneurs, and biotech venture capitalists.

Richard turned around. Near one corner of the room was his sharp-tongued attorney, Loretta Jacobs. Loretta took a sip from her dirty martini and smoothed out a wrinkle in her black suit. Sitting with the governor was Amy Baker. The governor knew her well, and apparently, she had asked to tag along.

Out of the corner of his eye, Richard monitored Amy's movement around the room. He smirked at Loretta, knowing she would intervene if the nosy reporter began pestering him.

The governor stretched out a hand toward Richard. "Dr. Hughes, I hear Monty's off to your alma mater this fall."

Richard flashed a satisfied grin. "Indeed. And this summer, he will be at the Brigham, shadowing some of the best physicians in the country."

"He will make a fine doctor. Inquisitive, tenacious, smart as hell." The governor nudged Richard with his elbow. "The apple doesn't fall far from the tree, huh? I'm sure he's being groomed to inherit the keys to the kingdom."

"Monty isn't sure what he wants to do yet."

"Well, he's got a lot to live up to."

Richard forced a smile. He thumbed Monty's note, which was folded up in his pocket. He lifted his chin toward the field. "We've got a great team this year."

At the bar, Elizabeth scanned the half dozen bottles of red wine.

"What can I get you, ma'am?" the bartender asked.

Elizabeth pointed to a bottle.

"Wonderful choice, Mrs. Hughes." The bartender poured a glass.

When she reached for the wineglass, she knocked it over. Wine spilled across the counter and dripped onto the floor.

The bartender rushed around the bar and snatched a towel from his waist. "I'll clean this up. Go enjoy the game. I'll bring you another glass."

Richard was watching the baseball game absentmindedly when Amy approached him.

Richard's eyes didn't leave the field. "Ms. Baker. I knew it was only a matter of time before you'd make your presence known."

"I wonder if you've considered Avastia's adverse reactions?"

He locked eyes with Loretta. "My lawyer, Ms. Jacobs, should have the answers to your questions."

Wearing a stern expression, Loretta stepped in between Richard and Amy. "Why don't you do everyone a favor and go get yourself a hot dog," she whispered.

Before she could respond, there was a knock at the door.

When a waiter opened the door, several FBI agents

poured into the room. Holiday shoved his badge in Richard's face. "Dr. Hughes, I'm an agent in the fraud division of the FBI, and I have a warrant for your arrest."

Richard's mouth opened, but no words came out.

Loretta grabbed the warrant from Holiday's hands. "On what charges?"

"The Department of Justice has filed a criminal complaint of research fraud," Holiday explained. "Dr. Hughes is accused of falsifying preclinical data, doctoring toxicology reports, omitting results about adverse events, and misappropriating clinical documents."

The governor stepped forward. "Is this about Avastia?"

"It's a fake, sir," Holiday replied.

Richard squeezed Monty's note in his pocket. He clutched his stomach in anguish, and his face turned ashen. As everyone watched, he fell to his knees, and his head hit the floor with a devastating thud. Richard saw a flash of white, and then a memory played like a movie in his mind's eye.

Richard was in medical school and had little time for anything but studying. And yet, somehow, he'd found an hour in his schedule to give Monty his first sailing lesson on the Charles near MIT. Richard was pleased to see his son eager to learn sailing and open to trying anything, even if he thought he might be bad at it at first.

It was a windy day, with gusts of 30 miles per hour, and Richard knew he'd have to teach Monty how to hike, a maneuver where a sailor extends their body off the side of the boat to keep it from tipping over. Richard explained the move to Monty before they put the boat in the water. Within minutes of leaving the dock, a gust filled the sail, and the boat tipped about 30 degrees. Demonstrating a hike for Monty, Richard extended his body over the side of the boat, stabilizing it. Afterward, the two switched spots so Monty could try the move when another big gust came.

When that gust filled the boat's sail, Monty did what his father had shown him. He leaned back and extended his back over the side of the boat. The boat began to stabilize, but Monty didn't have a firm enough grip on the rope and tumbled in the river. Richard quickly grabbed the boat's helm and looked over his shoulder to see his son flailing in the water. Other sailboats steered around Monty, nearly hitting him.

Richard steered the boat back to Monty and dragged his son into the boat. He covered Monty's shoulders with a towel and pointed the boat back to the docks. Something had shifted in Richard's mind that day. He'd realized the limits of his ability to protect his son. He hadn't been able to keep Monty safe. Something like this could never happen again. It was then that Richard decided that he'd do whatever he needed to do to keep his family safe.

Just before Richard lost consciousness at the feet of Agent Holiday, who'd come to take away his freedom, Richard realized that he'd overcorrected in his pursuit to ensure his family's safety. His initial healthy desire to protect Monty had become socially harmful. He'd rushed Avastia to market and ignored the warning signs along the way. All because he was convinced his drug would improve the health of the public—it was for a *good cause.*

Now, Richard was a cautionary tale for scientists and entrepreneurs, and a father who'd brought great shame to his family.

CHAPTER FIVE

Monty walked across the campus of Woodward Academy, which was about the size of three soccer fields. He passed dormitories, a library, and a sports facility that included a gym, indoor pool, squash courts, and rowing machines. Meandering paths wrapped around manicured gardens and wooden benches. He passed through a gate made out of a whale's jawbone and reached the main administration building.

Taking a deep breath, Monty pulled open a heavy oak door that had marble rings for handles. He walked into a long corridor that contained avant-garde sculptures in niches in the walls and a painting of Raphael's *The School of Athens*, which depicted the great philosophers Plato and his student Aristotle.

A few students from the ferry mingled in the lobby. By the wall, two security guards stood motionlessly. He walked over to the others and stood beside Edwin, who carried himself as the kind of privileged boy who started life on third base and thought he had hit a triple.

A woman with blond hair appeared on the second-floor balcony. She was wearing a black suit and an intense gaze. Her hands were folded behind her back.

It was Dr. Sonja Woodward.

The students looked up expectantly to the woman who would lead their reformation.

From the balcony, Sonja ran a hand over the shoulder of a marble sculpture of Michelangelo's *David*. "Michelangelo believed that every block of stone already had a statue in it and that it was the task of the sculptor to bring it out. He said, 'I have only to hew away the rough walls that imprison the lovely apparition to reveal it to the other eyes as mine see it.'"

Dr. Woodward walked down the stairs, running her hand along the railing. At the bottom of the stairs, she added, "You all are like blocks of stone. Our job at Woodward is to act like sculptors. Through specialized education, we will refine you. Remove unsound beliefs. Fine-tune your thoughts and deeds. Adjust your character. And, in time, cultivate virtuous behavior."

She led the students down a hallway, past pictures of US presidents, writers like George Orwell and T. S. Eliot, and philosophers such as Socrates and Marcus Aurelius. "Today, nothing prepares you to become moral citizens, and yet ethics must form the foundation of this nation. Our job is to help make you into principled leaders who can operate in society with the highest standards of integrity."

Head of Security, Mr. Aldrich, handed out a thick booklet to each student. "Everything you need to know about Woodward is in this handbook. They also contain your assigned roommate for the summer."

Monty opened his and found his name next to Edwin Thompson's.

"Mr. Aldrich will show you to the dorms," Sonja continued. "Inside your rooms, you will find letters with details about your community assignments. One of the most important aspects of your time here will involve internships in fields relevant to your future careers." Sonja raised her hands. "So, go to your rooms, unpack, and get to know each other. In an hour, join me and the faculty in the dining hall for dinner."

When Monty entered his room, Edwin was gingerly unpacking a framed cover of *The New Yorker*. The cartoon drawing displayed four couples dancing under starlight. Recalling that *The New Yorker* was known for "the best writing anywhere, everywhere," Monty assumed his roommate had literary ambitions.

"I'm Monty." He stuck out his hand.

Edwin shook it. Clean-cut and dark-haired, he smiled. "So here we are, plucked from our lives to participate in the great social experiment of our generation."

Edwin glanced at the envelope on his desk. "I'm interning at Nantucket's newspaper, *The Inquirer and Mirror*. I'll be working with this Pulitzer Prize-winning reporter named Amy Baker. She has a year-long Neiman Fellowship, doing a deep dive into the science of morality. Sounds like a thorn in Dr. Woodward's side."

Edwin eyed the envelope on Monty's desk. "What's your assignment?"

Monty tore open his envelope. "Nantucket Cottage Hospital," he said, unsurprised.

"A future doctor, eh?"

Monty shrugged. "Not really sure."

Jonathan Davenport sauntered in from the hallway. "Let me guess: Your dad was a doctor, his dad was a doctor, and probably his dad too?"

Jonathan shook hands with Monty and Edwin. "Anyway, you better figure out what you want to do with your life fast. It's too competitive to *not* know."

Monty shook his head. "I'm okay with uncertainty. Actually, I'm skeptical of anyone who's a hundred percent certain of anything, especially their choice of vocation."

The other two boys' faces looked doubtful.

Monty turned back to Edwin. "So you'll be working at the newspaper?"

"If it doesn't die in the forty-eight hours before he arrives," Jonathan snickered.

"Great journalism is still happening, even in the digital age." Edwin looked over his shoulder at the framed *New Yorker* cover on the wall. "I want to be an investigative journalist. I want to win a Peabody Award someday. I want to write about climate change, campaign finance reform, income inequality. Significant issues. These days, journalists are afraid to ask the tough questions. They don't keep leaders accountable. They write propaganda, telling stories that please the owners and advertisers."

It sounded ambitious to Monty, but noble.

"Can we lighten up?" Jonathan asked. "It's our first night." He shook his head. "It's all corrupt, anyway. It's the way of the world." He sat at Monty's desk. "My father was a lawyer at a major chemical company for two decades, then he became a vice president at the USDA."

"Is that even legal?" Monty asked.

Jonathan laughed to himself. "They call it the 'revolving door.' Perfectly legal to jump between roles, but is it right? That's a different question." His head swiveled around the room. "I guess we'll learn that here."

"This is boring," Edwin said. "Let's go meet the other students.

Edwin led Monty and Jonathan across the hall. They entered a room where a teenage girl with dirty blond hair was hunched over a laptop, absorbed in a video game, firing a pistol at zombies. The girl's bags sat unpacked on her bed.

Monty introduced himself.

"I'm Taylor." Her eyes never left the screen.

"What game are you playing?"

"First-person shooter. Takes place in the zombie apocalypse." She pointed to the teenage girl on the laptop's screen. "This little devil is Maeve. She just killed her brother."

"Why'd she do that?" Jonathan asked.

"Because it's the end of the world, dude. Because she was curious. Because she's a psychopath. Who knows, who cares. I'm gonna do something about it."

Taylor moved her character, a woman, toward Maeve, who was standing near a flower bed.

"What are you going to do?" Monty asked.

Taylor grinned. "We're just going to pick some flowers."

Maeve was holding a flower. "Please don't be mad at me," she said. "I'm sorry."

Taylor positioned her character behind Maeve. "Sorry ain't going to cut it." Taylor used the keyboard to point her pistol at the back of Maeve's head and whispered, "Just look at the flowers, Maeve."

"Well, here's an ethical dilemma," Jonathan said, leaning against the doorway.

Taylor fired the gun, and Maeve's body crumpled to the ground. "Solve the problem before it becomes a problem," she said.

Monty frowned. "It seems like Maeve regretted what she'd done. Isn't the guilt of killing her own brother punishment enough?"

"You would never be able to reason with Maeve," Edwin warned, "or rehabilitate her, let alone get her to feel sorry. You'd never be able to trust her."

"You'd always be worrying when she'd kill again," Taylor agreed.

"So you put her down for the safety of the community," Jonathan added. "The greater good, so to speak."

"And what about us? Can we be trusted? Can we be cured?" Monty asked.

Jonathan laughed. "Cured? I'm not looking for a cure." He glanced at his watch that displayed a running ticker of stock information. "If I had to worry whether each company I invested in was hurting sea turtles, I wouldn't make a dime."

Kirsten walked into the room. She was attractive and had straight brown hair. For the first time, the hood of her sweatshirt wasn't pulled over her head.

"Kids like us can't be cured," she said. "We had an honor code at my high school, but we all cheated. I couldn't keep up with all the homework. You think my parents would have accepted a B minus in AP English?"

"Moralists are always trying to improve humankind,"

Taylor complained. "Who says it needs improving?"

"If you deny our basic instincts, you deny what it means to be human," Jonathan added.

"I agree," said Edwin. "After this summer, we're supposed to be good little boys and girls? How are we supposed to change if Mom and Dad gave us naughty genes?"

"But most of us haven't even done anything wrong yet," Monty said.

"Most, not all." Cory strolled into Taylor's room, holding a football in his hand.

Jonathan nodded to the boy. "So what's your crime, Cory?"

"This year, I took the SAT for thirty-five seniors at fifteen hundred dollars a test."

"What did you score?" Kirsten asked.

Cory spun the football on his palm and grinned. "Near-perfect, every time."

"And it's the parents who pay, I'm sure," Kirsten said.

"Small price to pay to get your kid into the Ivy League," Cory replied.

Taylor switched off the video game. "Our high school participated in a radio contest where the most student votes got to have a famous singer at their prom. I created a bot that voted once-a-second, twenty-four hours a day, seven days a week."

"So you're a hacker?" Edwin asked. "Black hat or white hat?"

Taylor shrugged her shoulders. "Depends on the day."

"Did your high school win?" Jonathan asked.

Taylor pulled a cell phone from her pocket and scrolled to a picture on Facebook. The image showed Taylor with the pop singer Ariana Grande singing on stage behind her.

For dinner, the students made their way to Woodward's dining hall. Monty scanned the sprawling space. There was a massive stained-glass window at the front of the room. Chandeliers hung over several long oak tables.

"This is like Hogwarts for deviants," Monty joked.

Kirsten chuckled as she continued admiring a sculpture in one corner.

Mr. Aldrich instructed the students to seat themselves at any table. Monty, Kirsten, and Edwin took their seats at one table, and Cory, Taylor, and Jonathan sat at another nearby. Waitstaff crisscrossed the room carrying menus and steel trays.

"What's your story?" Monty asked Kirsten. "Has your genetic destiny materialized yet?"

"It depends on what you call breaking the rules," she said. "I'm a street artist."

"Like graffiti?"

"I just call it art, but sure." She opened a napkin and laid it on her lap. "Do you know Banksy's work?"

Monty did. The street artist's graffiti was called satirical and subversive. One of his pieces depicted two male English police officers holding and kissing each other. Another piece showed an English toll booth with an ax in its side. "Don't they call him the British vigilante?"

Kirsten nodded. "Sure, graffiti isn't technically legal, but it's still art. Banksy's a genius. An activist. Art collectors carve his graffiti out of walls and sell it for millions. I love the fact that while he has achieved international acclaim, his identity is still a mystery."

"Have you painted anything around Boston that I might have seen?"

"Did you see the mural of the pride of lions on the side of the Boston Public Library?"

"I'm guessing that wasn't a commission," Monty grinned.

Kirsten shrugged. "What brings you to this faraway island?"

Monty thought about his genetic test. His fake results. "I jaywalk occasionally."

Kirsten narrowed her eyes. "Rebel."

Monty turned to watch a dozen or so faculty members gather at a table across the room. Sonja sat next to Palmer. They looked like a brainy bunch. Tweed blazers, cardigans, and button-up shirts. The psychologists, anthropologists, and behavioral scientists had been plucked from the finest universities across the country. Monty had met plenty of academics during his internship at Nautilus over winter break. If he had to guess, these folks were discussing sleepless nights writing their dissertations or trading stories about their nightmarish postdoctoral experiences.

Waiters approached the tables holding notepads. The menu included fresh New England seafood: lobster, fried clams, crab cakes, Nantucket scallops, and clam chowder. There was also sushi and grilled swordfish. Monty ordered the lobster with chowder.

"Do you have chicken?" Cory asked.

The waiter smiled. "Whatever you'd like, sir."

Across the table, Taylor's face wrinkled. "You know these chickens probably lived in a windowless factory."

Kirsten threw her head back in disgust. "Vegans."

Taylor turned to Kirsten. "Scientists genetically

engineer the chickens' breasts to be so big, they can't even support their own weight."

Cory laughed. "What's wrong with oversized breasts?"

Jonathan chuckled. "Why couldn't Dr. Woodward have created *that* genetic technology?"

All the boys laughed. The girls were not amused.

Taylor handed her menu to the waiter. "Can you make a vegetable pita?"

The waiter smiled, nodded, and walked to the kitchen.

Sonja stood up from her seat among her colleagues. To get everyone's attention, she tapped her glass with a knife. "Good evening."

The dining hall grew quiet.

"You are the first class to attend Woodward Academy. You are an elite group from the finest prep schools along the East coast. Many of you will attend prestigious universities in the fall. Many will go on to found global companies or investment houses. You will have brilliant careers in business, law, engineering, and medicine. But before you do, we must address your predispositions."

"More like biological defects," Edwin whispered to Monty.

"Ticking time bombs," Taylor returned from across the table.

As the waiters carried food into the dining hall and set plates in front of the students, Sonja continued. "It is my view that you can work moral muscles just as you can physical muscles. We will spend the next three months doing just that. We may not be able to change your biology, but we can retrain it."

She smiled at Palmer and gestured for him to stand. "I will now turn it over to our psychiatrist and professor of philosophy, Dr. Palmer Reid."

Palmer kept his chin up, eyes forward, and held Sonja's gaze without looking away. His smile was confident, worry-free. Monty suspected his intelligence and independence had frustrated a few department heads during his academic career.

Monty sensed there was something about Sonja's personality—her philosophy, the genetic technology, Woodward Academy—that bothered Palmer. The way he chewed on his lip as she spoke, as if annoyed or in disagreement with her perspective.

"Is that the guy who lives on a sailboat?" Edwin asked.

Monty nodded.

Palmer stood and put his hands into his pockets. He scanned the students' faces as they silently picked at their food. "I bet you're all a bit overwhelmed right now. It's not easy to be the first to do something like this, and for that, I apologize."

Palmer raised his hand and paused for a few seconds. "What guides my hand?"

The students glanced at each other. No one answered.

Palmer's eyes sparkled. "My *mind* guides my hand."

"And my eyes guide my stomach," Edwin quipped, biting into a lobster roll.

Sonja glared at Edwin, but Palmer didn't respond. He appeared to be harder to rattle. Easygoing, almost bohemian. "If we train the mind, we train the hand."

Monty listened closely. The teacher's speech was heavy-handed but not self-righteous.

"We're not trying to replace your parents or your religion here. We're not trying to save anyone's soul. We're asking you to embark on a moral adventure. No one is born with moral character. It is something we *create*. It is hard learned. And like any expedition into learning, it is best to have a guide. We will be those guides for you on your moral adventure."

Back in Monty's room, Edwin watched the evening news on their room's flat-screen TV. The news opened with a story about severe weather in the southwest, then moved on to a story of sexual misconduct at a local business.

Monty used to watch the news every morning, but he'd recently switched to watching a travel show instead. Ever since, his mornings had become a lot more relaxed. "This stuff could give a Buddhist monk a panic attack," he said to Edwin.

Edwin glanced at a prescription bottle sitting on his desk. Monty followed his gaze and read the label: lorazepam. A medication for anxiety. "Without that medication, I'd probably be curled up in the corner sucking my thumb like a newborn."

"Why are teenagers so stressed out these days?"

"The pressure to succeed in school, and to get into Stanford or Yale or Harvard," Edwin said. "Advanced placement classes. Perfect SAT scores. Constantly comparing myself to my friends on social media. It ain't easy being a teen in the twenty-first century."

Monty had felt the same pressures. His future had been planned out: from high school, to Harvard, then to Harvard Medical School to study medicine. It was the same path his father had taken. The path he was supposed to—

required to—take.

Standing at his desk, Monty unrolled a poster of the painting *Wanderer above the Sea of Fog* by the landscape painter Caspar David Friedrich. The print depicted a man standing atop an exposed peak and looking out over a foggy mountain range. For Monty, it evoked feelings of wonder and adventure, but it also reflected his aimlessness.

A thousand paths ahead of him, but which one to choose?

Monty looked at Edwin. "Can we watch something else?" Edwin picked up the remote, but just then, the words *Breaking News* rolled across the bottom of the screen.

Amy appeared, standing in front of a building with large glass panels. "Amy Baker here, bringing you breaking news from Cambridge, where former CEO of biotech firm Nautilus Therapeutics, Dr. Richard Hughes, has just been arrested on charges of alleged research misconduct."

A picture of Monty's father was superimposed alongside Amy's image.

Monty closed his eyes. *It's begun.*

Amy continued. "It all began a month ago, when the *New England Journal of Medicine* accused Dr. Hughes of outright fraud. In the wake of these accusations, a special committee of the US Office of Research Integrity opened an investigation into the matter. They found that Dr. Hughes and his lead toxicologist, Dr. Iain Collins, had fabricated many aspects of the company's preclinical and clinical research studies, including dates and figures and the names of coauthors. In all, Dr. Hughes fabricated data in more than one hundred papers and nearly a dozen scholarly articles."

Amy stepped aside as an FBI agent walked past her pushing a cart that overflowed with binders and computer hard drives. "Effective at nine a.m. this morning, the board of Nautilus has asked Dr. Hughes to step down. This all comes just hours after Dr. Hughes announced his resignation as CEO, amid whispers concerning his physical health."

Amy skipped into a fast walk and caught up to the FBI agent. "Agent Holiday, if Dr. Hughes is convicted, do you know what kind of sentence he'll be facing?"

Holiday halted and stood up straight, looking like he was no stranger to the cameras. "A felony such as this carries a prison term of fifteen to twenty years. If these allegations are proven in court, the research community will never trust his work again."

"What happens now?" Amy asked.

"The FDA is re-examining Avastia's clinical trial data. The FBI's investigation will take months, perhaps years."

"But the drug stays on the market?"

"While it is under review, yes," Holiday said. "For now, the FBI has Dr. Hughes under house arrest. He's been banned from owning, operating, or directing a lab during the ongoing investigation."

The breaking news report ended.

Leaning forward at the edge of his bed, Edwin turned to Monty. "Where was Woodward Academy when this guy was in high school?"

Monty stared at his print of *Wanderer above the Sea of Fog*. Despite the news report, he wasn't thinking about his father. He was thinking about the coming summer here at Woodward. His future beyond that. His life.

"What if it doesn't work?"

"What do you mean?"

Monty's eyes scanned the room, settling on the ocean outside the window. "What if we're just inescapably bad, destined to end up like Dr. Hughes?"

Edwin laughed. "Then we'll end up wrecking everything we're involved in, I guess." He frowned. "Or maybe someone will put a bullet in our heads, like Taylor did to Maeve in that video game." He shrugged and stood up, walking over to Monty. "What's so riveting about this poster, anyway?"

"It represents an unknown future," Monty said.

Edwin shrugged again. "All I see is fog." He clicked off the lamp on his desk and leaped into bed.

Monty switched off his own light as he climbed into bed and tugged the covers up to his chin. Ever since he had learned about his father's fraud, sleeping had been a problem. Many nights, he would awaken abruptly and suck in air as if he couldn't catch his breath. Adrenaline surged, his body overheated, and he would kick off the covers in search of relief. Then he would stare into the darkness for hours as his thoughts spiraled.

He focused on the soothing sound of the crashing waves drifting through the closed windows. As he did, he realized he was exhausted from the day's events. His breathing slowed, and he drifted into a restless sleep.

CHAPTER SIX

One Month Ago

It was late when the knock came at the front door of the Hughes family home. That night, with his parents both upstairs, Monty hurried over to answer it and was surprised to find his father's lead toxicologist standing before him.

Dr. Collins's eyes were bloodshot. "I need to speak with your father, Monty."

Monty raised his eyebrows, certain Dr. Collins must have seen his father only hours ago at the party Nautilus had thrown in honor of the FDA's approval of Avastia. Shrugging it off, Monty stepped back and shouted up the stairs.

"Dad! Dr. Collins is here to see you."

Dr. Collins paced on the stoop.

Monty knew something was wrong. Dr. Collins was usually carefree, always quick with a joke. Tonight, his steps were quick and his fingers were twitchy. As he waited for his father to come downstairs, Monty leaned against the window. He could hear Dr. Collins mumbling on the stoop. When Richard appeared, he nodded to Monty as he left the house and greeted Dr. Collins in the driveway.

Kneeling at the window, Monty could see the two men and hear their conversation clearly.

"It's late, Iain."

"Did you get it?" Dr. Collins asked.

"Get what, Iain? It's ten o'clock at night."

"I emailed you the most recent toxicology report."

Richard checked his watch. "I'll look at it in the morning."

"The bromodomain inhibitors . . ." Dr. Collins kept his voice low.

Richard didn't say anything.

"The toxicology data shows that Avastia's off-target effects are toxic. Not just in animal models. *In humans*, Richard."

Monty squinted, still listening intently. He saw Richard run his foot through the driveway's gravel. "But Avastia hits all the druggable components, right?"

"It does interrupt gene regulators in healthy cells," Dr. Collins answered, "but my most recent report shows Avastia is toxic in liver cells, kidney cells, heart cells, and the brain."

"We'll do an independent study," Richard stammered out. "Restart the clinical trial. We must check and double-check our data to verify—"

"The show's over, Richard. The FDA will slaughter us when they see this report." The toxicologist scratched his cheek nervously. "Richard, I also found troubling discrepancies in our data. Some of the graphs and tables in the toxicology reports don't match up with the data in my original records."

Monty watched his father ask, "Are you suggesting the results were doctored?"

"That's exactly what I'm suggesting." Dr. Collins pulled a laminated folded from his jacket pocket and flipped to the third page. "I compared my toxicology results with historical data. I circled any places where my data didn't match the historical. There are a lot of goddamn circles, Richard!" He flipped to the last page. "This is my memo to the FDA."

Richard snatched the folder from Dr. Collins's hand. He scanned the text and read the memo aloud. "Toxicology studies show potent and systemic adverse effects, causing multiple organ failure in humans." He turned the page. "With regard to efficacy, attachment of DNA inhibitors was confirmed, but the strength of inhibition was negligible."

Monty's father lowered the report but said nothing.

"Don't you get it?" Dr. Collins asked. "Avastia isn't just unsafe. It doesn't even work." He looked dejected. "And our early trials were so promising." He exhaled sharply. "First thing tomorrow morning, I'll email this report and my memo to the lead reviewer at the FDA."

"You do that, and we're finished," Richard snapped. "We're at the point of no return. Trying to stop now would be like shooting a BB gun at a freight train."

"If we stay in market with Avastia, we could hurt a lot of people."

Richard shook his head. "You need to look at the bigger picture. This wouldn't just destroy the company you've spent five years building; it would destroy your career. No lab would touch you after this." Richard hesitated before speaking carefully. "Need I remind you that you're one of the company's largest stockholders? Do you really want to throw away millions in stock options?"

Richard handed the report and memo back to Dr. Collins and led him to his car. "This is all just numbers on a screen right now. Go back to the lab, remove the outliers, and discard the experiments that don't validate safety or efficacy. We'll work out the kinks in future trials."

Richard was telling Dr. Collins to fabricate data. To lie. He had always told Monty that they weren't conducting basic research at Nautilus. Their work wasn't about the thrill of scientific discovery. Nautilus was a publicly traded company with a strong profit motive. With so much money at stake, so many careers on the line, was his father right?

Monty watched Dr. Collins step into his car, knowing that the toxicologist would make the data say what Richard needed it to say, and that was decidedly troubling. But what could he do? What *would* he do?

"This is only temporary," Richard told his toxicologist through the window of the car. "Avastia worked in clinical trials. We can sort out the off-target effects later. We just need to stay on the market. The company needs to recoup that billion dollars it took to research and develop this drug."

"You can stop sweet-talking me, Richard." Dr. Collins stared up at Monty's father. "I want five million on top of my annual salary."

"Hush money?"

"If that's what you want to call it."

Richard nodded decisively. "I'll have the money wired

into your account by the end of business tomorrow."

"What should I do now?"

"Go back to the lab and make the data sing."

Dr. Collins wrapped his fingers around the steering wheel and nodded unconvincingly.

Richard walked back to the house, and Monty scampered into the kitchen, hoping to make it look like he'd been making a sandwich. Through the window, he watched Dr. Collins drive away.

Richard entered the kitchen and eyed the bread and slices of turkey on the counter. "Can I have one, bud?"

Monty cleared his throat and asked, "What did Dr. Collins want?"

"Just double-checking some numbers."

Richard took his sandwich and headed upstairs. Before Monty could do the same, bright lights flashed through the kitchen. Looking out the window, he saw Dr. Collins drive back up the driveway. Monty opened the door and locked eyes with him. Dr. Collins pulled a packet of paper from his pocket and slid it into Monty's hand. He leaped off the porch and glanced back at Monty, then got into his car and sped away.

Monty closed the front door and listened for signs of movement from the floor above him. Using the flashlight on his cell phone, he skimmed the pages the toxicologist had given him: Dr. Collins's memo. Monty examined the circles showing where the data had been doctored. Their frequency was staggering.

In his bed on Nantucket Island, Monty sucked in a panicked breath.

For a few seconds, he thought he was still in Chestnut Hill, struggling with a revelation that was now a month old. Why hadn't he made Dr. Collins's report public? Had he kept quiet because of family loyalty? It was one thing to consider "doing the right thing," but it was quite another to turn your father over to the FBI. When it's blood, right versus wrong wasn't so cut and dry. Perhaps he just didn't have the courage, Monty thought. None of it mattered, though. The truth had come out somehow.

Doesn't it always?

Monty put on a jacket and walked outside into the brisk Nantucket air. A thick mist had enveloped the campus. He strolled into a courtyard lit with soft blue lights and stared into the bubbling fountain at its center. Then he turned and ambled to the ocean shore, where he stared out into the crashing waves. In the distance, he could hear the faint sound of a foghorn.

When you love someone who's done something terrible, do you stop loving them?

CHAPTER SEVEN

Sonja walked down a long hallway in Moralis Laboratories. Medical journals featuring company scientists hung along the red brick walls. The labs she passed were filled with marble-topped benches covered in notebooks, Petri dishes, and bottles full of colored chemicals.

Sonja turned a corner and saw Edwin's parents sitting in two chairs outside of her office. Mrs. Thompson stepped forward eagerly and cupped her hands around Sonja's. The woman looked starstruck, and Sonja reminded herself that she had achieved some level of fame. Nothing made her happier than to know that her school held such promise in the eyes of others.

Mrs. Thompson adjusted her stylish cat-eyed glasses. "We're so glad you could find time in your schedule to meet with us, Dr. Woodward. Nothing seems to work for Edwin."

This type of meeting hadn't been presented to the prep school superintendents or congressmen. From the perspective of a politician or a school administrator,

Woodward Academy was a no-brainer. *Solve a problem before it becomes a problem.* But not all parents had been eager to ship their children to Sonja's summer science experiment. If someone's child inherited problematic genes, what did that say about the parent? Most parents, though, welcomed the intervention. Many had long been managing their children's behavioral issues. For people like the Thompsons, Sonja was their only hope.

Mr. Thompson folded his tweed jacket over one arm. "We weren't exactly surprised when Edwin tested positive."

"Edwin's plagiarism case at school was so embarrassing for us," Mrs. Thompson added. "We're good parents. We taught him right from wrong."

"Maybe military prep school would have been better for him," Mr. Thompson said. "Something more regimented, more disciplined."

"We were so relieved when we heard he'd been accepted to Woodward," Mrs. Thompson continued as though her husband hadn't spoken. "We were even happier to know that there are *other* options available."

Sonja stood and gestured toward the door with one hand. "Let's go into the lab. I want to show you the alternative."

The parents followed her into a lab space. The stinging scent of antiseptic hung in the air, along with a faint hissing as the room maintained its negative air pressure. Sonja stopped in front of a bulky machine that sat on one bench. The device held four inverted test tubes.

"As I said over the phone, this device would be a last resort, reserved only for those students who don't respond to our curriculum."

The parents curiously bobbed around the machine.

Mrs. Thompson cleared her throat. "What is it?"

"This is CRISPR technology." Sonja pressed a button on the back of the machine, and it hummed to life. "It allows us to target genes with great precision and turn them off or on at will."

Mrs. Thompson fiddled with one of her pearl earrings.

Recognizing the need for clarification, Sonja turned to meet the mother's eyes. "Think about a tomato, Mrs. Thompson. There are genes that code for a tomato's redness, but if we used CRISPR to silence the 'red' genes in a tomato, it would lose its color."

"How does this relate to my son, Dr. Woodward?" Mr. Thompson asked.

Sonja nodded. "Our genes code for eye color, height, intelligence, but there are also groups of genes responsible for complicated traits involving human behavior, including one's capacity for empathy. CRISPR technology allows us to turn on what we call the 'empathy genes.'"

Mrs. Thompson looked at her husband.

"It's entirely safe, I can assure you both."

Sonja knew the Thompsons didn't understand the technical details, but it didn't matter. They just wanted to know that Edwin wouldn't humiliate them again. A highly educated scientist wearing a white lab coat was telling them that their son could be "fixed," and that was all they needed to know.

At that moment, Palmer entered the lab. He was wearing a defiant grin. "That's right. Just switch a few of Edwin's genes on and, presto, he's cured."

The Thompsons looked at each other, then at Sonja.

Sonja spoke quickly to manage the damage control.

"You'll have to excuse our resident psychiatrist. Dr. Reid favors the humanities over the sciences."

Palmer shook his head. "Human beings are more than their genes." He turned to face the parents. "If you don't mind, could I ask you some questions about Edwin?"

The mother shrugged. "If you think it will help."

Sonja clenched her fists, but she couldn't justify interfering now.

"Did Edwin show a lack of empathy in childhood?" Palmer asked.

Mr. Thompson didn't need long to find an answer. "Edwin used to steal toys from his friends, and he never seemed to feel guilty about it."

"At what age?"

"Throughout his childhood," Mr. Thompson answered, "but it began around four or five years old, if I had to guess."

"That age is typically when we see a child's sense of morality develop—their understanding of right and wrong." Palmer tilted his head. "How about your household, Mrs. Thompson?"

The mother glanced at Sonja, startled. "What do you mean, Dr. Reid?"

"Any physical or psychological abuse? Did the two of you ever separate? Did either of you abuse alcohol or suffer from mental illness? What losses did Edwin experience in his early life?"

Mr. Thompson grunted, looking unimpressed. "Why is any of this relevant?"

"It's important to understand the developmental conditions to which Edwin was exposed. Adverse childhood experiences have been linked with negative mental and physical health outcomes in adulthood."

The father wrapped his arm around his wife, pulling her close. "We don't look into the past too much in our household, Dr. Reid."

"Provided it's not causing any dysfunction in one's life, I think that's fine, but Edwin has behavioral issues. After looking at his medical history, I see that he's suffering from anxiety. With such dysfunctions, we can usually follow a thread back to trauma in early development."

The father turned to Sonja. "What's happening here? What good is any of this?"

Sonja stepped forward. "I'm afraid it's getting late." She led the Thompsons to the door where Mr. Aldrich was waiting. "I appreciate you both visiting and considering this option. Mr. Aldrich will lead you out and drive you to your hotel."

"Do you think Dr. Reid could be right?" Mrs. Thompson asked. "That we need to examine events from childhood?"

Sonja shook her head. "You'll have to excuse Palmer, Mrs. Thompson." He has trouble knowing where the education ends and the medicine begins."

"We love our boy," Mr. Thompson said.

Sonja placed a hand on his shoulder. "We'll take good care of Edwin."

As the parents left, Palmer waved. "A pleasure meeting you both."

Sonja held her smile until the Thompsons turned a corner and disappeared. Then she spun around and glared at Palmer. "Never challenge me like that in front of parents. It was unprofessional, and it undermines my authority."

Palmer didn't appear intimidated. "We won't help these kids if we don't address the root causes of their problems."

"Save the lessons for the classroom, Palmer. We're under a lot of pressure to make sure this program works. You think this lab, this school—*your job*—will be around if this first batch of students doesn't respond to the curriculum?"

Palmer let out a deep sigh. "These students are more than their predispositions."

Sonja raised a hand to silence him. "Just focus on your lesson plans, Palmer. If we don't see progress in the classroom, we will fix the problem in the lab. And, if that time comes, I will call on you, Dr. Reid."

"I'm an academic, not a scientist."

"You're a medical doctor, a licensed psychiatrist, are you not?"

Palmer nodded, gritting his teeth.

"If I tell you to throw the switch on this machine, you will do it."

"Why do you want me to administer the treatment?"

"You'll establish bonds with these kids," Sonja said. "They'll trust you, and that makes you the best man for the job."

CHAPTER EIGHT

Richard blinked his eyes open. Half his vision was taken up by the ceiling, the other half by a television that lay beyond the end of his bed. The television was playing CNN, and the text at the bottom of the screen read, *The biggest fraud in the history of modern science.*

A blurry hospital room with sterile white walls came into focus. The bed he lay in was partially upright, and an IV trailed from his arm. The rhythmic beeping of machinery echoed the pulse beating in his ears.

He pulled his blanket up and saw a plastic object fitted just above his ankle. As he realized where he was, the memory of his arrest rushed through him. At Fenway, he had been approached by a federal agent, an Agent Holiday, and then he'd passed out. Through a window in the door, he could see a man standing guard.

The door opened, and Elizabeth stepped into the room. Her face was pale, her eyes puffy and red.

Richard pushed himself up in his bed. "How long have I been out?"

Elizabeth wouldn't meet his eyes. "Twelve hours, maybe."

Richard reached out his hand, but she didn't move.

"I'm so sad, Richard, so ashamed. I wish I could just run away."

"But you didn't."

She shrugged. "You're still the man I fell in love with when I was twenty-three. The man I built a life with. Raised Monty with. Thought I would grow old with."

Richard had been disgraced, but he knew Elizabeth wasn't going anywhere. Their roots were too deep. But he also knew Elizabeth had become accustomed to an upper-class lifestyle. Elite gym and golf club memberships. The credit cards in her Dolce & Gabbana pocketbook. The sailboat. The glamorous parties with Boston's elite. Was she really going to give that up in her sixties? Ride the subway now? Work out at a regular gym for $45 a month?

Elizabeth approached the bed and slid her hand into his.

Richard smiled in relief. "I was going to tell you and Monty after the game."

"About your illness?"

"Everything."

Loretta strode into the room.

"I'm so glad you're here," Richard said. "What kind of trouble am I in, Loretta?"

The lawyer moved to stand beside Elizabeth. "A special panel within the FDA is reviewing the data on Avastia. They want to pull the drug off the market as soon as possible. The SEC has filed civil and criminal investigations against you, and there are currently two class-action lawsuits."

She offered Richard a stern look. "You're lucky I'm a founding partner of the best law firm in Boston. Otherwise, we'd be talking inside a federal prison, separated by glass. I got the judge to agree to house arrest because of your medical condition."

Elizabeth squeezed Richard's hand.

Loretta opened the binder in her hands and flipped through the documents within it. "Since the *New England Journal of Medicine* published accusations of fraud against you, I suggest we file a defamation lawsuit against the journal. It'll cost a few million dollars."

Richard waved one hand in agreement.

"When is the trial?" Elizabeth asked.

"In sixty days."

"Will he go to jail?"

"I can't keep him out of prison, Mrs. Hughes. The scope of this fraud is enormous. The prosecution is asking for the full amount of prison time allowed. It's possible I could lessen it, but not likely."

"What's the number?" Elizabeth asked.

"Twenty-five years minimum. I might be able to get it cut down to fifteen."

What's the difference? Richard knew his condition was terminal—he probably didn't even have six months to live. He likely wouldn't even make his trial. *Ironic*, he thought. *A cancer biologist with terminal pancreatic cancer*.

Elizabeth leaned against the window, gazing down at the park below.

A doctor entered the room. His jacket read Christopher Schoenfeld, MD, but otherwise, he didn't introduce himself. He didn't even lift his eyes from the medical chart in his hands as he addressed Richard.

"Last year, we surgically removed tumors from your abdomen. The scans now show that the cancer has returned and metastasized. Your liver is full of tumors, and your kidneys are failing."

Dr. Schoenfeld finally looked up from the chart and locked eyes with Richard. There was contempt in his eyes, which he didn't bother to hide, and Richard suspected his next words before they left his mouth.

"A few days ago, I would have prescribed Avastia, but that seems a bit risky now, don't you think, Dr. Hughes?"

Elizabeth stepped away from the window. "We can try surgery again, right? Chemotherapy? What about radiation?"

Dr. Schoenfeld shook his head. "Your husband's cancer is too far advanced. He probably won't make it to the end of summer, if I had to guess."

"But there must be experimental trials." Elizabeth turned to Richard. "With your network, Richard, how could you not get the best treatment?"

Richard looked away. "You think my colleagues will answer my calls now?"

"The most difficult part of my job is telling patients I have no more treatments to offer," Dr. Schoenfeld said. "I'm not having that problem with you."

Richard understood the doctor's disdain, but the comment shocked him. "What about the Hippocratic—?"

"You took the same oath, Dr. Hughes, yet you broke it by creating your fake drug. Who knows how many patients your actions will harm."

Dr. Schoenfeld closed the medical chart and approached the door. "I'm discharging you today. If I weren't wearing this coat, I'd throw you out onto the street myself."

Richard knew he deserved the doctor's contempt. He was a scientific criminal now, like the infamous scientist who'd wrongly linked vaccines with autism. He felt shame in every corner of his body. In his stomach, deep in his bones, on every breath. His greatest passion in life had been practicing science, and he'd never be able to do it again. There was no coming back from what he'd done.

Why had this happened? Richard thought. How had everything gone so terribly wrong? How had he let himself cross so many lines? He thought about his evolution from medical school to scientific research. Richard had learned while studying to become a doctor that he didn't enjoy working with patients. To him, patients were messy, their conditions hard to diagnose, sometimes impossible to treat effectively. The data on his computer screen could be controlled, though. Data didn't complain like a patient. Data couldn't send him anxious messages if discomfort cropped up. Data didn't lie. At heart, Richard was an experimentalist, not a clinician.

Richard had only ever wanted to be a basic scientist. To follow his curiosity, not solve practical problems, like finding a cancer cure. He wondered if he'd lost his way when he became an *applied* scientist with a biotech company that had a profit motive as well as a board and shareholders to please. The transition from basic research to scientist-businessman had all happened so fast. The early data showing Avastia's potential. The building of a company. The heady experience of thinking he could rid mankind of the scourge that was cancer.

And now, everything Richard had built was on fire.

CHAPTER NINE

Standing at the front of his classroom with his hands in his pockets, Palmer posed questions to his students. "What does it mean to flourish in life? What does 'the good life' mean to you? What kinds of habits, traits, behaviors, or ways of thinking help you thrive in society?"

Letting his students contemplate his questions, Palmer realized he was doing exactly what he was born to do: teach. Even though Woodward Academy was a place of experimentation, and he didn't always see eye-to-eye with Sonja, Palmer thought they shared a similar hope that their efforts might make for a better society.

Sonja believed that technology could help achieve that aim. Palmer was of a different mind. He thought he could make things better through lessons and discourse. A great teacher, like the one Palmer aspired to be, aimed to enlighten students by pushing them to grapple with difficult and sometimes morally challenging ideas. This was the mandate Sonja had given him when she first approached him to teach at her school. Potentially subjecting his students to an experimental genetic technology hadn't been in the job description.

Palmer pointed to one of the students sitting near the back of the classroom. "What do you think, Jonathan?"

"The almighty dollar," Jonathan offered.

The other students chuckled knowingly, and Palmer nodded.

A legitimate answer.

"For some, accumulating money fulfills many psychological needs and certainly plenty of practical ones too." Palmer scanned the class. "What else?"

"It's hard to live the good life if you're sick or hurt," Cory said. "I injured my back in a football game last season. For weeks, all I could think about was the pain."

Palmer agreed and explained that good health was the foundation upon which a flourishing life was built. "What else?"

"Power," Edwin answered.

Palmer nodded, then explained the philosopher Friedrich Nietzsche's belief that seeking power was the driving force in humans. "The will to power, so to speak."

"What about pleasure?" Taylor added. "Playing video games is my happy place."

Palmer walked down an aisle and told the class about Freud, who thought that the main psychological needs are fulfilled by seeking pleasure and avoiding pain.

"For me, the *good* life is about creative expression," Kirsten said. "When I'm drawing or making graffiti art, I'm totally immersed, in the zone."

Palmer explained the work of psychologist Mihaly Csikszentmihalyi, who argued that the more time people spent in a "flow state," the happier they were.

"What about meaning?" Monty said.

Palmer was pleased with Monty's remark. He sat on the side of his desk at the front of class and told the students about Victor Frankl, who wrote his famous book *Man's Search for Meaning* while imprisoned in a concentration camp during World War II. For Frankl, the primary drive of humans was to find meaning in life.

Palmer used a marker to write *Happiness* on the board at the front of the classroom. He pointed to a bust of the philosopher Aristotle that sat on a nearby bookshelf. "It was Aristotle who proposed that our actions and choices are driven by one question: Will this make me happy?"

Palmer let that sink in for a moment before continuing. "What if I gave each of you a billion dollars? You could do anything with the money. What would you do? Would you buy a house or a boat, take an around-the-world trip?" He gestured to a notepad that sat on every student's desk. "Write them down and put them in order of priority."

After thinking briefly, students began scribbling on their notepads. Palmer walked the aisles, occasionally hovering over a student as he or she wrote. Palmer noticed that Monty seemed to be having trouble. He was tapping his foot and staring at his desk distantly, unable to produce a list.

"All right, stop," Palmer said and returned to the front of the room. "We all have different ideas about what might make us happy. One person may want to build a family, another an empire. Some pursue wealth, health, power, praise, or creativity. Now, ask yourself: Why do I want these things?" He scanned the room. "Will these things produce feelings of happiness? Perhaps, but only temporarily. The feeling would fade."

Palmer walked behind his desk. "If you compare the subjective feelings of happiness of someone who won the lottery and someone who's been paralyzed from the waist down, one year after each event, there's no difference in their perceived levels of happiness. This is called hedonic adaptation. Humans can adapt to almost any circumstances."

"But what creates long-lasting happiness?" Palmer turned to the whiteboard to write "the true source of happiness is virtue."

"What does virtue even mean?" Kirsten wondered aloud.

"Doing the right thing?" Monty offered.

Palmer nodded. "We could sum up all religion, theology, and philosophy in those four words."

"'Right' and 'wrong' are completely subjective," Edwin said with a shrug.

Palmer erased his previous words and wrote: *The Golden Mean.*

"According to Aristotle, the 'right' choice is the middle point between two extremes. The golden mean is somewhere between excess and deficit. Virtue is therefore the natural result of continually making choices within the golden mean. And this leads to happiness."

"Consider courage," Palmer offered as an example. "What's an excess of courage?"

"Carelessness?" Taylor said.

"I was thinking of recklessness, but that's great," Palmer replied. "What's a *lack* of courage?"

"Apathy?" Kirsten tossed out.

Palmer nodded. "Or paralysis. If you found yourself in a dangerous situation, what might be a response at the midpoint between recklessness and paralysis?"

"Bravery," Monty said.

"Exactly," Palmer replied. "It's not second nature to make choices within the golden mean, but it can become a habit with training. Over time, such conditioning leads to character, which then leads to moral virtue.

"To expand on Monty's earlier point, you could say that the goal of ethics is to 'do the right thing, with the right motive, in the right way.' This leads to happiness according to our friend Aristotle, who suggested that only a life of virtue would make a person truly happy. And a life of virtue comes from making a habit of choosing the golden mean.

"Now, I don't want to overload you with formal instruction this summer. During my classes, most tests will be in the form of essays, which will help promote reflection and self-examination. We will learn by engaging in rigorous self-study and living what Socrates called 'an examined life.'"

Ending the class, Palmer pointed to a stack of books at the back of the room. "On your way out, grab a copy of Aristotle's *Nicomachean Ethics*. For tomorrow, please read the first three chapters from book one. There will be an essay evaluation at the start of class."

CHAPTER TEN

On the shuttle to Nantucket Cottage Hospital, Monty leaned against the open window beside him and breathed in the salty air as he passed marshes. He saw people walking along boardwalk trails and picking at food while sitting at outdoor picnic tables.

Several miles from Woodward, he watched shorebirds fight over scraps of fish on a remote beach. Out on the water, a sailboat banked in the stiff breeze. They drove past houses with weathered shingles and people relaxing on their front porches.

The shuttle settled near the hospital's emergency room entrance. Monty joined a group of a half dozen teenagers. Like Monty, they appeared to be recent high school graduates, some of whom perhaps also had the goal of becoming healthcare providers.

A physician in his fifties wearing a light blue-colored shirt under a white coat approached the group, introducing himself as Dr. Edward Sax. His jet-black hair was slicked back.

"Welcome to the hospital's emergency room," Dr. Sax said in a flat tone. "The ER is the tip of the spear. It takes quick thinking and a strong stomach to hack it here."

Monty scanned the bustling emergency room and its controlled chaos. Nurses shouted commands, patients writhed and whimpered in their exam rooms, doctors quickly scanned charts to make fast but educated decisions. Monty felt his senses sharpen. The ER was a long way from the sleepy labs of Nautilus Therapeutics.

"Right now, you're all guppies," Dr. Sax continued. "You don't know anything. In fact, you don't even know what you don't know." He pointed to one of his ears. "You've got two ears and one mouth. Why? So you can listen twice as much as you speak. This summer, I won't be teaching biology or chemistry. You'll learn that in college in the fall. What I will be teaching you is how to deliver patient care—how to *listen* to patients—with compassion and empathy.

"What is the first rule of medicine?"

No one said anything.

"'First, do no harm.' That is our credo." Dr. Sax scanned the students. "Who can tell me what it means?"

"Don't screw up," a teenage girl joked from the back of the group. Monty recognized her from Woodward Academy, but they hadn't met.

"It means that, as clinicians, we have the power to cause harm." Dr. Sax led the students down a busy hallway, sidestepping two nurses who were wheeling a gurney out of an elevator. As the gurney passed, he glanced down at the woman lying on it; her eyes were pinched shut in agony. "Most patients who visit the ER are having the worst day of their life. They're at their most vulnerable. It is our obligation to avoid causing them any more pain or suffering."

Monty wondered if Dr. Sax thought Woodward students were a liability. Did he think he would have to watch Monty more closely during the shadowing program? Was this "great power, great responsibility" lecture meant for the Woodward kids?

Dr. Sax funneled the students into an exam room. He fiddled at a counter and then slapped an X-ray against a lit screen on the wall. Monty recognized a chest cavity. He'd examined plenty of chest X-rays at Nautilus with his father.

"Does anyone know what we're looking at?" Dr. Sax asked.

"Lung cancer," Monty said. "Stage four."

Dr. Sax's eyes widened. "Treatment options?"

"Surgery, radiation, chemotherapy," Monty offered.

"Tried, failed," Dr. Sax replied.

Monty thought about Avastia. Has Dr. Sax seen the news about his father? Was he still prescribing Avastia? The drug wasn't technically off the market yet.

Dr. Sax led the students into a nondescript room full of computers. He then excused himself, handing the students off to a man who worked for the hospital's IT department, who helped the students register for their hospital identification cards.

The next day, Monty ran down a narrow dirt path alongside Edwin, Cory, and Taylor. He tugged at his tight-fitting polo, which had the words *Woodward Academy* written across the left side of his chest. The students were jogging to the Woodward boathouse, which was about two miles away from the campus, on Pimnys Point.

It was required that all students participate in a sport. Monty and his fellow joggers had chosen rowing, though Cory would've preferred football had Woodward offered it. In his packet, Monty had found a daunting list of rowing terms the students were asked to memorize.

"What's 'catching a crab'?" Monty asked as they ran, swatting away a mosquito.

Taylor, who never missed a reading in class, was quick with an answer. "It's sticking an oar in the water and not being able to release it. The oak jerks up fast, hits you in the chest or face, and ejects you from the boat violently."

"Twenty bucks says Cory catches a crab." Edwin jabbed an elbow into Cory's side.

Cory laughed and shoved Edwin, nearly toppling him.

The students gathered at the edge of the ocean, where several two-person rowing boats bobbed in the water under the hot midday sun. A handsome slender man in his mid-forties appeared from the entrance of the boathouse. He strolled onto the beach, his light-brown boat shoes skimming over the sand. His frayed white jeans were rolled up above his ankles.

"Call me Coach Bode," the man said calmly. "I'm head of the Nantucket Rowing Club. I'll teach you how to row this summer." He ran a hand through his salt-and-pepper hair. "I will teach you how to work hard and how to work together as a team. If nothing else, this intense exercise will help you blow off steam while your teachers shove philosophy down your throat."

Coach Bode rolled his pants up farther and waded into the water. He ran a hand softly, tenderly, along the boat's surface, then gazed out over the ocean. "There's nothing like surging through the water at twenty miles an hour, in sync with seven other athletes. The feel of your oar catching water. Your lungs burning as you pull. Your legs on fire."

Monty glanced at Edwin, who rolled his eyes, but Monty rather liked the coach's romantic sensibility. Coach Bode seemed pure and kind, if a bit innocent.

"If you're lucky," Coach Bode continued, "you'll get a feeling called 'swing.' The best rowers call it a sensation of near perfection, a state in which all athletes move in harmony with no wasted energy."

He faced the students and pointed to the list of rowing terms in Edwin's hand. "I hope you've memorized your terms. Getting a boat from the boathouse out into the water with your crew requires coordination, a defined sequence of steps. Each action in the sequence has a specific term and purpose. We lift together. We carry the boat to the water together. The oars go in the boat first. We enter the boat in pairs. Understand?"

Coach Bode raised his voice. "My job is to get you ready for the Nantucket Regatta in two months. It's a rowing competition between elite schools from Boston and Nantucket High School nearby. It happens here at Pimnys Point. Today, we're going to practice in two-person boats, so please choose a partner and go find a boat."

Monty glanced at Edwin, who shrugged.

Fifteen minutes later, the students were 20 feet off the shore inside their boats. Coach Bode followed close behind in a motorboat. Monty and Edwin were propelling their boat through the ocean, in sync. The other students, including Cory and Taylor, rowed behind them. Coach Bode shouted commands through a loudspeaker. "Catch together, row together. Stay synchronized!"

The soft spray of ocean water was refreshing in the summer heat. From behind, Monty watched Edwin's oar catch the water at the same time as his. In sync, the boat accelerated.

Edwin faltered and leaned to the right abruptly. The spoon of his oar missed the water, his weight shifted, and the hull of the boat lurched to the left. Monty couldn't get his oar out of the water before the blade was pulled under at a steeper angle and the handle rammed into his chest. The fierce motion drove the air from his lungs and knocked him back violently. He saw a flash of white as the world turned. Then his ears were ringing as he struck water and sank below the surface.

Perhaps it was Coach Bode shouting orders through the loudspeaker that reminded Monty of his father at that moment. When he was six years old, his father had taken him to Brigham and Women's Hospital, where he had worked as an oncologist during his residency. He'd been a doctor in training, working 100-hour weeks.

Monty would never forget how bone-crushingly tired his father had looked that day. There had been dark circles beneath his eyes, his eyelids sagged. Monty had thought he might break into tears. That day, Monty had accompanied his father on a few visits with patients. So exhausted, it had seemed a challenge for Richard to stand. The nurse had left the room after one visit. To treat a patient's seizure, Richard had intended to administer 20 milligrams of diazepam. Instead, he'd accidentally administered 20 milligrams of Lasix, a diuretic used to treat fluid buildup due to heart disease. He only realized the mistake an hour later while restocking a shelf in the pharmacy with drugs. Richard scratched the back of his head.

Monty wrapped his arms around his father's leg. "Is everything all right, Dad?"

Richard stared at a box of Lasix. "I made a mistake."

"What kind of mistake?"

"I gave a patient the wrong medication."

"Will they be okay?"

Richard glanced toward the room, where they could see the patient sleeping in his hospital bed. "If something was going to happen, we would have known by now."

"Should we tell somebody?"

Richard shook his head. "What good would that do?"

"I don't get it."

Richard bent over. "The patient wasn't hurt." He shrugged. "No harm, no foul."

Monty remembered feeling confused that day. The incident seemed more complicated than how his father had chosen to see it. No doubt fatigue played a role in Richard's mistake, but had it influenced his choice to keep the incident to himself? Was it unethical to act if nothing had happened? Even though the patient hadn't been harmed, should Richard have told the patient or reported the incident to the hospital? What was the "right thing to do" in this situation? In any situation? Monty thought it wasn't always easy to determine right versus wrong.

Monty inhaled deeply as his face broke the surface of the water. He felt two arms wrap around his chest. In a daze, he heard Edwin's voice saying "I got you, buddy," and felt himself being pulled into Coach Bode's boat.

Around 11 o'clock that night, Monty winced while shifting positions at his desk in his dorm room. It still hurt to breathe, hurt to move. He didn't want to think about what could have happened if Edwin hadn't pulled him out of the water after the accident. He hadn't seen him since the incident.

Thinking perhaps Edwin was outside, Monty left their room and walked across the campus, enjoying the cool, salty breeze on his face. The beam from the lighthouse lit a wooden path to the ocean. In the distance, Monty could hear the crash of waves and the squawks of seagulls as they glided over the surface of the water.

Monty spotted Edwin on a manmade jetty, holding a golf club. Edwin lifted the club over his head and swung through a golf ball. The ball sailed out into the black sky. Likely hearing Monty approach, Edwin said, "Wait for it . . . wait for it . . ." There was a faint plunk as the golf ball landed in the water.

Edwin threw his arms upward. "Ah, man! Missed."

"What are you aiming for?" Monty searched the distance.

Edwin lifted his chin toward a sailboat. *Palmer's sailboat.* Apparently, his teacher had gotten the boat in good enough condition for him to spend the night out on the water.

Edwin took a long inhale off a joint and exhaled smoke slowly.

"Isn't that Dr. Reid's boat?" Monty asked, surprised.

"Perfect distance for my chip game," Edwin quipped.

Then he lifted the golf club toward Monty. "Take a few whacks."

Monty waved a hand dismissively. "Golf was never really my sport. Too much like life."

"How's that?"

"Boring."

Edwin chuckled. "Well, judging from today's performance, rowing isn't your sport either."

Monty coughed into his hand. "By the way, Edwin, about th-that. I, uh . . . wanted to thank—"

"Don't worry about it, man." Edwin pressed the club into Monty's hands and stepped back, holding the smoking joint between his fingers. "These golf balls aren't going to hit themselves, you know."

Monty took a practice swing on the wooden jetty. The movement sent a sharp pain down the left side of his body, and he hissed.

Monty steadied himself. Trying to avoid any conversation about the pain, he asked, "You know what makes someone a great golfer?"

"Tell me, oh wise one."

Monty laughed, then said, "Good or bad, he never lets the previous shot affect how he approaches the next one. He can wipe the slate clean before each shot."

"You have wisdom beyond your years, Mr. Hayward."

Monty laughed. "Dr. Reid better watch out. I'll have his job in a few years."

Edwin bent over and placed a golf ball on the tee. "All right, buddy, let her rip."

Monty lifted the club up and over his shoulder. Grimacing, he rotated his hips through the pain and swung through the ball hard. The club struck the golf ball awkwardly, and it traveled about ten feet, skipping across the water.

Edwin offered Monty the joint. “Swing lube.”

Monty waved away the offer and placed another golf ball on the tee. He took a few practice swings. In class, Palmer had said they could learn a lot about people by playing golf with them. Did they cheat by moving the ball after a poor shot? Palmer had told them that when playing golf, most people had an ethical problem with picking up their ball after a bad shot and moving it to a better position. However, they were less conflicted about using their feet to kick the ball or moving it with their golf club.

In the latter, there was more distance between them and the action. They didn’t use their own hands, so they felt less “involved,” less responsible. Parallels of this could be seen in certain nightmarish historical events, such as the Holocaust. Palmer told them that bureaucrats in Hitler’s regime who worked at desks and directed prisoners to death camps on paper were nowhere near the people they were condemning to death. Because of the distance, they felt less involved. The prisoners were numbers on a page.

Monty’s next swing sent the ball maybe a hundred yards in a straight and low trajectory. It was a near-perfect strike.

“Nice one.” Edwin reached for the club. He squinted into the darkness, preparing for his shot. “You know, Monty, you strike me as a guy who always plays his shots where they lie.”

“I scored a positive on Dr. Woodward’s genetic test, just like you. Just like everyone else.”

Edwin peered at Monty suspiciously. “Yeah, I can’t

argue with that." He turned and centered his body over the golf ball. Taking a deep breath, he pulled back the club and hit the ball cleanly. The ball disappeared into the sky.

Monty waited to hear a splash.

What he heard was the golf ball hit wood.

"Oh, crap! We hit Dr. Reid's boat!" Edwin yelled.

"We?" Monty said, already crouching low.

A light went on in the sailboat.

Monty and Edwin sprinted back to the dormitory. They dashed into the hallway, panting heavily, and then broke into laughter.

"Hey, man, thank you for doing what you did earlier today. For saving me."

Edwin turned right down their hallway. "We're roommates. We have each other's backs." He smirked. "Make sure to back me up if things go sideways for me."

Edwin knocked on Jonathan's door. "Let's see if anyone's up."

"I need to get some rest. I'm waking up early to study for that quiz before class tomorrow," Monty said.

"I'm getting up to study early, too." Edwin opened Jonathan's door. "I'll wake you up."

Monty bit his lip. "Okay."

Jonathan was leaning forward in his desk chair. The two monitors in front of him were filled with scrolling numbers. Jonathan didn't turn his head when the door opened. "Not now, I'm trading." His eyes were narrow with concentration. "I've got seventy-five thousand on the line right now." He sipped from an energy drink and reacted to something on the screen with wide eyes. "No!" He grabbed his hair with both hands.

"How much did you lose?" Edwin asked.

"Twenty grand." Jonathan popped up from his chair. "Whatever. It's my father's money, anyway." He used a remote to unmute the TV. "Commercial break is over. You guys watch this show?"

Monty had seen *American Greed,* a show about Americans who had fallen prey to scams or fraud. Someday, they'd no doubt make a show about his father.

Jonathan raised the volume. "Let's see who the jerk is tonight."

It was always the same story, Monty thought. Some financier type with wildly high ambition starts a business. Maybe they're running a legitimate operation at the start, but then they get greedy and begin stealing money from clients. With all the extra cash, they live the high life for a while, party incessantly, buy cars, houses, boats.

But then maybe the market turns, or they suffer a financial loss and they can't recover. Clients ask for their money, but the con men can't come up with it. They realize their operation is going to collapse, and they just can't give up. So they continue to lie, cheat, or steal, burying themselves further. The scheme unravels, and they get caught.

Monty thought about his father's mistakes. He thought about how con men like his father always seemed to think they wouldn't be caught, but even the most charismatic and intelligent con men eventually went down, but not, tragically, before ruining the lives of hundreds, sometimes thousands of people.

Jonathan sniffed the air close to Edwin, then sniffed again. "Someone smells nice." His voice dripped sarcasm. "New cologne?"

Edwin pulled the half-smoked joint from his jacket

pocket. "Want some?"

Jonathan pulled a flask of whisky from his desk. "More of a drinker myself." He took a swig, then handed the bottle to Edwin, who took a pull from it. Edwin's face scrunched up as he swallowed. He handed the bottle to Monty, who reluctantly took two sips, then handed the bottle back to Jonathan.

Jonathan grabbed his copy of *Nicomachean Ethics* from his desk. He lifted the bottle with one hand and the book with the other. Mocking Palmer, he asked, "What's the golden mean for the consumption of this whisky? What's the right amount to drink, given my weight, gender, where I'm from, who my parents are?" He took a swig. "All these principles, rules, standards. People are wound too tight around here."

Edwin agreed. "What's so 'good' about being good? Where's the advantage? What Dr. Reid calls 'doing the right thing,' I call 'losing the edge.'"

Monty considered that. "I think Dr. Reid is saying that 'doing the right thing' is its own reward, right? If we cheat, break the law, lie, steal, or whatever, even if we get away with it, we would still know we did something wrong. Our consciences wouldn't be clear. We'd feel shame or guilt, even if only subconsciously. Dr. Reid's saying that being virtuous leads to a clear conscience and a happier life."

Rhythmic footsteps sounded faintly from the hallway. Jonathan rushed to the door. He turned around, his eyes wide with fear. "It's Dr. Woodward!"

The boys spun around in circles, trying to figure out what to do. Then Monty grabbed the copy of *Nicomachean Ethics*. He gestured for Jonathan to sit at his desk and open his notebook. He waved Edwin to the bed.

There was a knock at the door. "It's past curfew," Sonja said. "What are you boys doing?" The door opened and Monty began reading aloud.

"One swallow does not make a summer, neither does one fine day; similarly one day or brief time of happiness does not make a person entirely happy."

Sonja looked stern as she entered the dorm room, but her expression soon softened into a smile. "I'm glad to see you boys studying together." Her eyes bounced from Monty, to Edwin, to Jonathan, each of them holding their backs stiff. "I want you all back to your rooms and in your beds immediately."

The door closed, and the three boys exhaled deeply. After a moment, they began laughing.

CHAPTER ELEVEN

Richard let his head hang while an orderly pushed his wheelchair through the hospital's hallways. Elizabeth and Loretta walked along beside him. Nurses and physicians mingled throughout the halls, glaring at Richard as he was wheeled past.

When they came out into the hospital lobby, they found the media waiting for them. Dozens of reporters formed a circle around Richard and rattled off questions. Loretta pushed cameras and tape recorders out of Richard's face and gestured for the orderly to keep moving.

One reporter shouted, "Dr. Hughes: Why didn't you make your cancer public?"

Another yelled, "Do you regret what you've done, Dr. Hughes?"

"Did your wife or son know about the fraud?"

Beneath the onslaught of frantic reporters, Richard's senses began to spin.

"This is being called the greatest crime in scientific

history," another reporter shouted. "What do you have to say to that?"

"Dr. Hughes, do you have anything to say to the patients who have been harmed by Avastia?"

The reporters surrounded them. Loretta stopped walking and faced the cameras. "Ladies and gentlemen, Dr. Hughes is very sick. I ask that you please give us space. Once we have settled in at Dr. Hughes's home, we will issue a formal statement—"

"I just want to say," Richard cut in, never pulling his eyes from the floor, "I'm terribly sorry for the pain I have caused. I just want to spend time with my family—"

"Is it true that your wife turned you in to the authorities?" someone asked.

Richard snapped his head up and around to search Elizabeth's face. He met her eyes and she looked away. Then she shot the reporter a hostile look.

Richard chose to believe what the reporter had said. *How could she—*

Elizabeth grabbed the handlebars of Richard's wheelchair and pushed it forward, forcing the reporters to make a path.

"Are you going to leave your husband, Mrs. Hughes?"

"Get the hell out of my way!" Elizabeth yelled.

In Chestnut Hill, the Hughes house had become part prison, part hospital. Guards stood vigil throughout the house, roamed the driveway and lawn, and sipped coffees in unmarked cars on the street. From where he sat,

Richard caught the eyes of one guard, and he knew he would never again have privacy.

The walls are listening now.

The living room resembled a hospital room and had an empty bed in the center. Near the window, Richard slumped in his wheelchair, feeling haggard and weak. He watched nurses install equipment around his hospice bed.

His deathbed.

Richard could no longer lay claim to the National Medal of Science that was displayed in a glass case on the wall. Everything he had earned in his career was being systematically stripped from him. Editors would retract his published papers from their journals. He would be kicked off scientific advisory boards. There would be no more keynote speeches, no more appearances in PBS documentaries, no more invitations to the White House. Anticipating his physical death, he could feel the sickening weight of a social death pressing down on him.

"Dr. Hughes?" One of the nurses patted the mattress of the hospice bed. "Your bed is ready for you. Would you like me to help you?"

Richard stared at the nurse. "I'm not getting into that goddamn bed."

CHAPTER TWELVE

Monty rolled over, rubbed sleep from his eyes, and peered across his dorm room. When he found Edwin reading at his desk, Monty frowned and grabbed his cell phone to check the time. *7:45 a.m.* Shit! Palmer's class began at eight, and Monty hadn't read the chapters for today's writing exercise.

"Rise and shine, buddy." Edwin closed his copy of *Nicomachean Ethics*. "Almost time for class."

Monty sprang out of bed. "Why didn't you wake me up?"

Edwin shrugged. "After last night, I figured you could use some extra z's."

Monty pulled on some jeans and a T-shirt. It was difficult not to curse Edwin for allowing him to sleep in. "Screw you, man. You said we'd study together this morning."

"Easy, easy," Edwin said.

Monty shook his head and hurriedly stuffed his backpack with a notepad and his copy of *Nicomachean*

Ethics. "Whatever, it's fine. You ready?"

"Let's get our philosophy on," Edwin said.

The two left the dormitory, rushed across the courtyard, and minutes later, entered Palmer's classroom. Most of the students were sitting quietly in their seats, staring at their phones. Monty took a seat, unloaded his backpack, and nervously began tapping his pen against the desk.

"Morning, class." Palmer walked into the room with a stack of blue notebooks under one arm. "I hope you all enjoyed your reading last night."

He walked the aisles, placing a notebook on each student's desk. "Inside these booklets, you will find a sheet of paper with three questions based on the reading you've done." With the notebooks distributed, he looked at his watch. "Please choose one question. You will have a half-hour to write." He pressed a button on his watch. "Please begin."

Monty flipped open his notebook.

1. *What is Aristotle's "Doctrine of the Mean"?*
2. *In what ways does the Greek concept of eudaimonia differ from our modern-day concept of happiness?*
3. *How does Aristotle define moral responsibility?*

Monty scanned the room with dread. Most students had begun writing; even Edwin was scribbling away. Monty closed his eyes to think of something, anything, but he was stuck. Then he thought about his father. His fraud and arrest. The example he had set for Monty, for others.

Monty set his pen to the paper and wrote without restraint, an almost torrential output. He filled the first page, then the second. He wrote and wrote and wrote.

What happens when your hero, your role model, turns out to be a fake? The person you looked up to for wisdom and direction? What happens when they commit an unthinkable crime? What happens when that person is your father? No longer a master of the universe. Not a builder, but a destroyer.

Now he's sick. Dying. And here I am, trying to make sense of the shame as he falls from grace. And what do his actions say about me? My tendencies? My future? He's my father, blood. What does that make me capable of? Most people never face a terrible dilemma. In class, Dr. Reid calls it "moral luck": When you go through life without having to face some moral dilemma. What if I'm not so lucky? What will I do when I reach a crossroads? An impossible decision.

Everyone says they would speak up. Do the right thing, follow their conscience, but how can you know until it happens? History is littered with good people violating their consciences. Because they couldn't stand up to authority. Because they couldn't disagree with a group. Richard Hughes, the great man, just couldn't admit that, for the first time in his life, he had failed. And it led to his own undoing.

Monty stopped. He set his pen down and shook his head. What was he doing? The words he was writing were too honest, too revealing. A confession. If he submitted this writing, his cover would be blown. Surely, Palmer would tell Sonja, and nothing good could come of that.

Monty scribbled out his dad's name, crumpled the

paper into a ball and started writing on a new page.

Thirty minutes after they'd begun, Palmer stopped the students and dismissed the class. When he reached the teacher's desk, Monty set his notebook on top of the others. Just before leaving the room, he tossed the crumpled pages into the trash.

Shortly after class, Palmer was rushing to keep up with Sonja as she raced through a hallway of Woodward. She occasionally glanced to either side at the classrooms they passed. "I have a meeting in fifteen minutes, Dr. Reid. Give me the shortened version, please."

Palmer cleared his throat. "Right now, the students are undergoing standard psychological assessments."

Sonja peered through one window. A half dozen students were seated in the classroom, including Monty and Edwin. At the front of the classroom stood Palmer's research assistant, Jessica. She was wearing a white lab coat and read from a clipboard.

"Which test are they taking?" Sonja asked.

"They just finished The Matrix Experiment."

Palmer tapped on the window to get the attention of Jessica. She opened the classroom door and handed Palmer a piece of paper.

"Here are the students' results, Dr. Reid," Jessica said.

"Thank you, Jessica."

She closed the door and returned to the front of the classroom.

"Matrix Experiment?" Sonja said. "Remind me what

that is, please."

"Jessica just gave the students twenty math problems. They're relatively easy to solve, but we only give them five minutes to solve them. It's impossible to solve them all in that amount of time, but they solve as many as they can, and after time expires, they physically insert their exams into a shredder at the front of the room. Then they *verbally* report their scores to Jessica. Obviously, they can choose to report their actual scores, or they can lie."

Palmer scanned the paper in his hand. It contained two columns of numbers: one for the actual score and one for the reported score.

"I remember this experiment now," Sonja said. "The shredder only shreds the sides of the paper, leaving the test area intact, right?"

"That's right. The experimenter gives each student a dollar for every correct answer they report. On average, about seventy percent of people who take the Matrix Experiment don't report their actual scores. They generally report a score one or two questions higher than their actual score. We call this 'small cheating.'"

"Why only report one or two above their actual score?" Sonja asked.

"It's about as much as their conscience will allow before they start to feel guilty for lying. If given the opportunity, most people bend the truth, but they'll only go so far before they start to feel bad about doing so."

"How did the students respond?" Sonja asked.

Palmer scanned the list of students. "It looks like most students reported scoring about two or three more than their actual scores." He ran his finger down the paper. "Taylor got a five and she reported a seven. Jonathan got an eight, he reported an eleven. Cory got a three and he reported a seven."

"Any big cheaters in the group?"

Palmer's eyes grew wide. "Edwin reported a score of seventeen."

"A near-perfect score? That's impossible, right?"

"It looks like he actually scored an eight. That definitely puts him in the 'big cheater' category."

"As you know, the Thompsons are concerned about Edwin." After a moment, Sonja added, "What about Mr. Hayward?"

Palmer ran his finger down the list of names. "Monty reported a score of ten."

"And his actual score?"

"Ten."

"Interesting."

Palmer led Sonja across the hall and pointed into another classroom. "We're about to repeat The Matrix Experiment with this other group of students. However, before they take the test, these students will be asked to write out the Ten Commandments on a sheet of paper. Studies show that getting students to recite an honor code just before an exam encourages ethical behavior and dramatically reduces cheating."

"Why's that?"

"Reading the Ten Commandments activates their conscience."

They continued down the hall and Palmer used his keycard to open a door. He led Sonja into a large room that had a glass wall separating it from a classroom. On the other side of the glass, a psychologist held up cards displaying different inkblots for Kirsten to see. A speaker on their side of the glass allowed Palmer and Sonja to hear what Kirsten said she was seeing for each inkblot.

"Psychological testing," Palmer said.

"Will the results be ready for next week's staff meeting?" Sonja asked.

"Once I collect the raw data, I can create the report quickly."

"Anything you can report now?"

"Many of these students had rather troubling experiences during their childhoods."

Sonja waved one hand dismissively. "Congress doesn't care about spankings and bed-wetting, Dr. Reid."

Palmer stared at Sonja. "Experiences like humiliation, physical abuse, and neglect can have wide-ranging implications for these students' future psychological and physical health."

Sonja glanced at the clock on the wall. "Anything else?"

Palmer gritted his teeth but didn't object. "Monty's an interesting young man. I looked at the results of his psychological testing before our meeting. He doesn't show the same antisocial behavior as Edwin, for example. It seems like Monty's problems are more existential. He's dealing with shame. This was displayed in his projective assessments, but it also came through in the essay he wrote about his father, who seems to cause him trouble. The essay was brilliantly written—the best in the class."

"Do you have a diagnosis, Dr. Reid?"

"In my field, we talk a lot about empathic failure. It occurs when a young person's emotional needs aren't adequately met. I think that's what happened to Monty."

"And how do we help him evolve?" Sonja asked.

Palmer shook his head. “I’m not sure yet. But I can tell you this: Monty wants to be here. He wants to heal.”

CHAPTER THIRTEEN

Monty walked through the automatic doors into the emergency room at Nantucket Cottage Hospital. He passed several exam rooms, his head on a swivel, until he spotted Dr. Sax speaking with another doctor.

"You're late," Dr. Sax said. Before Monty could reply, the doctor pointed back toward the exit. "You're riding in the ambulance with the paramedics today."

Monty turned to see the lights of an ambulance flash on. "Better hurry," Dr. Sax added. "They're heading out on a call now."

Monty ran through the exit doors and knocked on the ambulance's passenger-side window. The paramedic pointed to the back of the truck. "Jump in!"

Monty circled the truck, entered through the back doors, and buckled himself to a bench next to an empty stretcher. The ambulance roared to life and left the hospital.

A panel of glass at the front of the truck slid open, revealing a balding man in the passenger seat. "We're heading to the house of an elderly woman on the other side of the island. The call said shortness of breath. She's got lung cancer. Her name's Linda Caldwell. Been in and out of the hospital over the past six months."

Several minutes later, the ambulance pulled into the driveway of an old house. Monty followed the two paramedics up to the front door. One was carrying a green-colored oxygen tank; the other, a large red bag of medical supplies.

Monty's heartbeat accelerated. He was about to enter a house to care for a stranger in distress. It was a rush, but anxiety and uncertainty danced along his nerves as well.

The paramedics knocked on the door. It opened quickly to reveal a young woman, perhaps 19 years old, with blue eyes and dark curly hair.

"She's over here on the couch," the young woman said.

She led the paramedics to the couch, where an old woman was lying lengthwise, breathing shallowly. One of the paramedics slipped an oxygen mask over Mrs. Caldwell's mouth and nose and started the flow of oxygen. She took deep breaths.

Monty looked around the room. The interior of the house had a nautical theme. A whale's jawbone hung on one wall. The mantle over the fireplace was decorated with seashells and lighthouses. A copy of Herman Melville's *Moby-Dick* sat on a coffee table.

As the other paramedic rifled through the medical bag, Monty looked over at the young woman, who was watching the paramedics take care of her grandmother. He was intrigued by her long, curly brown hair and the strong and dignified way she held herself, even in an emergency. Her sundress showed a slender and fit body.

Monty wanted to learn from the paramedics, but he felt drawn to her.

Casting about for a reason to talk to her, Monty saw a framed picture of a man standing in front of a dead whale on a beach that looked like it belonged in Nantucket Harbor. "Who's the man in that picture?" Monty asked the young woman.

She seemed relieved to have something to distract her worry. "My grandfather," she said. "He was a whaler here in Nantucket."

"Do you live on the island?" Monty asked.

"I'm just here for the summer, spending time with my grandmother before . . ." She hesitated, watching the old woman struggle for air. "She doesn't have many options at this point."

"My name's Monty."

"Laura." She glanced at the couch worriedly.

Monty noticed a notebook in Laura's hand. "What's that?"

"Hoping to fill it with poems this summer."

Just then, the old woman went limp.

Laura leaned closer and gripped the edge of the couch. "She passed out. What's wrong? Help her!"

"She has a pulse," one paramedic said, "but it's weak. We need to get her to the hospital. Right now." He ran out to the ambulance to get the stretcher while the other paramedic packed up the medical supplies in a hurry.

The first paramedic rolled the stretcher through the door, and the two men lifted the old woman onto it. Then they were out the door, wheeling the stretcher to the ambulance, where they loaded it into the back. Monty and Laura were soon seated beside it and they watched a paramedic insert an IV into the woman's arm. The ambulance started and sped off. Through the window between the back and the cab, Monty watched the ambulance weave past cars and cut through intersections.

"Oh, no," The paramedic said. "Cardiac arrest."

Laura turned to Monty, her eyes wide with confusion.

"She's having a heart attack," Monty said.

The paramedic powered up a defibrillator and grabbed the paddles from the machine. He applied gel to the paddles and opened the woman's shirt. Just as he was lowering the paddles to her chest, the driver looked back through the window.

"What are you doing? You can't shock her!"

"Damn!" The paramedic lifted the paddles. "That's right."

"What do you mean?" Laura demanded. "Help her! She's dying!"

"We can't," the paramedic holding the paddles said. "She has a DNR."

"What?"

"Do not resuscitate. Legally, we can't do anything." He put the paddles back on the machine. "We have to respect her wishes."

Laura began crying and shaking in her seat. "Please, do something."

Monty watched the old woman's face turn blue. He looked back at Laura, who was sobbing with her head in her hands. The paramedic hadn't turned the machine off.

Monty remembered the five-week emergency medicine course he'd taken one summer where he'd learned how to use a defibrillator.

Monty didn't let himself think; he snatched the paddles

off the machine, pressed them to the woman's lifeless chest, and delivered the charge to her body.

The paramedic snatched the paddles out of Monty's hands and looked down at the woman. Her lips were turning a pinkish color. Quickly putting the paddles away, the paramedic pressed his fingers to her neck.

He frowned at Monty. "She has a pulse."

Laura threw her arms around Monty.

The paramedics wheeled the elderly woman into Nantucket Cottage Hospital, where she was examined by ER physicians and admitted into the hospital for monitoring. Saying nothing, the paramedics escorted Monty to Dr. Sax's office.

"Resuscitating a patient with a DNR is a very serious matter, Mr. Hayward. A DNR is a legal order for us to withhold CPR in the event of a cardiac event, just like the one that happened today." He shook his head knowingly. "I knew it was a risk to accept a student from Woodward. I should throw you out of this program."

"I couldn't watch her die," Monty said.

"Sometimes, it's not our right to make that choice. Mrs. Caldwell made her decision when she signed the DNR."

"But why wouldn't she want help in that situation?"

"She lost her husband over the winter. She's very ill. She's lost the will to live. As doctors, we might not want to give up on our patients, but we also have to respect their wishes."

Dr. Sax shook his head and leaned back in his chair.

"You disobeyed a legal directive, but the patient isn't raising the issue." He shuffled some papers around on his desk. "You can go now."

CHAPTER FOURTEEN

Holding a stainless steel pole hooked to an IV, Richard looked out the window of his house to see his street crawling with reporters, cameramen, and press vans. Inside the house, furniture had been wrapped in plastic, possessions were packed in boxes, and the walls had been stripped of artwork.

Richard scanned family photos on the fireplace mantle. He had pleaded with the FBI to leave the pictures of summer days on Nantucket with Elizabeth and Monty. Another captured the day Monty learned how to sail in Boston harbor. His favorite showed Monty on the deck of their Nantucket home as the sun set. He wore a dark blue sweater, and he had his feet on an ottoman while reading a novel.

On a bookshelf, Richard's eyes landed on *Mountains Beyond Mountains* by Tracy Kidder. The book had inspired him when he was a medical student. Monty had displayed the same idealism as the book's subject, Paul Farmer, a physician who had spent his career advocating and caring for the sick and those in poverty around the world. He had intended to give the book to Monty to read over the summer, but he hadn't seen him since his arrest at the baseball game.

From the dining room, Richard heard Loretta talking on the phone with prosecuting attorneys. He knew the Massachusetts court would deny him the right to sue for defamation; it was a long shot. What did it matter? He would die in prison, anyway.

Once she'd hung up, Loretta entered the living room. "I just got off the phone with the prosecutor—"

"How long is the sentence?" Richard interrupted.

Loretta paused and observed Richard for a moment. "They're going to press for the full sentence. Medium-security prison. Not Club Fed, but not maximum security, so you're lucky there. Right now, I'm trying to protect your assets. Most of your possessions will go to auction. The attorneys will go after your life insurance policies to pay back any patients who might have been hurt."

Richard buried his head in his hands. He would have liked to give Monty something, but even a book might not be worth it. Not now. Not when he was missing. "Will I be able to leave anything to Monty?"

"I don't expect anything to be left over for an inheritance."

Loretta sat in a chair beside the hospital bed and crossed her legs. "I understand that you haven't been able to get a hold of your son, Richard. Before we met, I had my own corporate intelligence firm. We did 'fact-finding.'"

"A private investigator?"

Loretta nodded.

"Can you help me find Monty?"

Loretta didn't hesitate. "I can get started right away."

Through the window, Richard watched her wade through a crowd of reporters. They pressed tape recorders into her face as she stepped into her BMW.

When Loretta was gone, Richard wheeled his IV toward the kitchen. He tried to avoid eye contact with Holiday, who was supervising his team, but the agent stepped in front of Richard before he could enter the kitchen.

"My grandmother lost her life savings in the Madoff scandal," Holiday said. "Instead of retiring to watch cable television while working on puzzles, she bags groceries at a Whole Foods for income. But faking a cancer drug? That's a new low for a white-collar criminal. I'd put Avastia in your IV, if I wasn't an FBI agent."

Not knowing what to say, Richard wheeled around Holiday. He crossed the living room and hesitated at the entryway to the kitchen when he saw Elizabeth sitting at the kitchen table, spinning her wedding ring around her finger. Her eyes were red and puffy, wet with tears.

Elizabeth wiped her eyes, slipped her ring off, set it on the table, and stared at it. "None of my friends will return my calls. I saw Nicole at the Shops at Chestnut Hill yesterday. We used to get drinks at the Cheesecake Factory all the time. When she saw me, she just turned around and went down the escalator."

Richard sat down at the table and set his hands on top of Elizabeth's. "Where's our son?"

She didn't lift her eyes from the table.

Richard pulled Monty's note from his pocket and slid it in front of Elizabeth. "Monty knew about the fraud," he said. "Why would he leave, though? We gave him everything. Everything I did, I did for him."

"We both know that's not true, Richard."

"I didn't come from some wealthy Bostonian family. I fought for every inch of my success, and I'm proud of how far I've come. And so what if I didn't hug Monty before bedtime? So what if I didn't tell him I loved him every day? He knew I loved him."

Elizabeth raised her eyebrows. "Did he?"

"My father didn't even pay attention to me. I did the best I could, all right?"

Elizabeth burst into tears. "How could you do this to us? We had everything we could've ever wanted. Now we have nothing. Not even our son."

Elizabeth stood up and walked toward the stairs.

"Where are you going?" Richard asked.

"To take a nap. I'm exhausted."

Richard glanced at the wedding ring, which still lay on the table. "Aren't you forgetting something?" He picked up the ring and pressed it into her hand.

Elizabeth wiped tears from her face. "I'm all alone, Richard. I just want to go somewhere where I won't be followed by the press. I don't think I can stand to see you in court. To see all those people look at you with hatred."

"What are you saying?"

"You have advanced cancer. You don't have much time." She fixed her gaze on the floor. "Maybe you could go sooner. I could go with you."

Still holding her hand, Richard tightened his grip on her wrist. He understood what she meant. "I'm not going to do that, Elizabeth. *You're* not going to do that, either."

Elizabeth sniffed loudly, then walked up the stairs, her head lowered.

Richard watched her disappear around a corner and heard their bedroom door close behind her.

CHAPTER FIFTEEN

By July, the students had worked through most of *Nicomachean Ethics*, studying the golden mean and other ethical principles. Palmer's teachings stressed experiential learning, case studies, and real-life situations, and he was always asking, "What would you do?" His classes were always the most thought-provoking, but Monty found that other teachers were also broadening his perspective.

A lover of science, Monty hadn't spent much time engaging with the humanities. He felt more comfortable on the field trip to a wildlife refuge discussing Charles Darwin's theory of evolution and the diversity of birds on Nantucket. It was nonetheless interesting, though, to study ancient wisdom and lessons from the world's religions. A historian asked students to read the Indian spiritual text, the *Bhagavad Gita*. They also read the novel *Siddhartha* by Herman Hesse, and they learned about the Buddha and how he achieved enlightenment.

One teacher, a sociologist, quoted from the Jewish Talmud: "That which is hateful to you, do not do to your fellow. That is the whole Torah; the rest is the explanation." Other teachers delivered aphorisms that have worked for centuries. "Love thy neighbor," "don't cheat, covet, steal, or kill," and, of course, the Golden Rule.

At the beginning of each class, Palmer typically had the students do ten minutes of mindfulness meditation, during which students closed their eyes, focused on their breathing, and let their thoughts float into and out of their consciousness. Afterward, Monty felt more relaxed and reflective, more open to new ideas and points of view.

Palmer also introduced the students to self-compassion meditation, which allowed the students to send kindness to themselves. With their eyes closed and their bodies laid out on yoga mats on the floor, the students whispered such phrases as "May I be gentle with myself," "May I know that I am a good person," and "May I know that I am enough." The practice, Palmer explained, would help the students feel better about themselves and less reactive to the normal ups and downs of life. He cited research that suggested that self-compassion meditation increased well-being and helped lower the risk of anxiety and depression. Palmer even showed them how to perform Tai Chi.

On a sweltering summer day, Palmer kicked off another class by pointing to Edwin. "Let me ask you a question, Mr. Thompson. Would you say you are a better-than-average driver?"

Edwin looked around the room and then shrugged. "Yeah, sure, I think I'm better than average."

Palmer looked at Taylor. "What about you?"

"I went across the country with my family one summer. I drove all the way from Arizona to California. So yeah, definitely better than average."

Palmer nodded. "In social science research, there is a theory known as illusory superiority, in which people overestimate their own abilities in relation to others. Most people think they are better-than-average drivers, better students, or better athletes."

Palmer folded his arms behind his back.

"Most people also believe they are more ethical than others. We like to think we are good people. We like to think we'll make sound ethical decisions in school or work, but that overconfidence can lead us to make decisions without reflecting on our ethics. This can be problematic if we are facing psychological or organizational pressures.

"See, most of us want to act ethically, but we also want to please authority figures. For example, we might have a boss who asks us to do something that doesn't align with our ethics. We also have a natural desire to be part of a team. Sometimes, we can be so focused on advancing a team's goals that our behavior departs from our own ethical standards."

Palmer pulled up a presentation and scanned the faces of the students. The image on the screen showed a man being accosted by paparazzi on the streets of New York City.

"This is Bernie Madoff," Palmer narrated. "In 2008, he was responsible for the largest Ponzi scheme in history."

A cameraman was shoving Madoff, trying to bait him into reacting violently, or saying something incriminating. Madoff was lifting one finger at the man, urging him to back off.

"How did this scandal happen?" Palmer asked. "Why do you think Madoff did it?"

Palmer glanced at Kirsten, who was drawing quietly at her desk. "Kirsten, stop sketching, please. "Why do you think Madoff did it?"

"He's a psychopath," Kirsten said without looking up.

"Go deeper," Palmer replied.

"Maybe he was one of those misguided people who admired greedy villains in movies," Jonathan offered, "instead of seeing them as cautionary tales."

"Greed likely played a role," Palmer agreed. "What else?"

At that moment, Monty thought of his father. Richard shared a lot in common with Madoff, a man who had spent his entire life winning. When Richard discovered that Avastia was a failure, he'd made up some numbers. Perhaps he had thought of it as a bandage that would buy him time to create a long-term solution. But the solution had never come, and the initial lie demanded more covering up, until it became a runaway train.

"Maybe he couldn't admit he'd failed," Monty said.

"Very good, Monty," Palmer said. "When Madoff realized his business might fail, he lied to cover up his mistake. Research shows that we dislike losses twice as much as we enjoy gains. This is called loss aversion. People will take more risks to avoid losing the things we have than we would have taken to get them. Instead of admitting an embarrassing failure, Madoff engaged in fraud."

Palmer scanned the room. "Things will go wrong in your lives. We can't win at everything. When you stumble, you can hide from yourself and others or you can face your failure. I recommend the latter."

The next photograph showed a space shuttle. The

following showed it exploding in midair. "This is the *Challenger* shuttle," Palmer said solemnly. "It exploded after launch in the eighties."

Palmer advanced to a picture of a command center filled with NASA engineers. "The engineers here knew that the shuttle's O-rings could fail at lower temperatures. The day of the launch was cold, so they knew the O-rings might be vulnerable. In fact, the engineers voted that they should cancel the launch."

"Then why did the launch happen?" Cory asked.

"Shortly before the launch," Palmer explained, "the engineers' supervisor reminded them how much money they had invested into the launch and convinced everyone to continue. The engineers didn't resist their supervisor. They stayed silent. They conformed."

Palmer continued. "This is called groupthink. It's a very real pressure to do and say what your friends, peers, or colleagues do or say. We take cues from others. We want to fit in. This natural impulse can lead groups to make decisions against their better judgment. This is what happened in the *Challenger* explosion."

The presentation then showed a short video of Adolf Hitler marching with soldiers in a parade, his hand raised in salute. The video advanced to heart-wrenching photographs from the Holocaust—horrific images of corpses stacked in piles within a Nazi concentration camp.

Palmer was solemn. The series of images didn't need an introduction.

The next image was a portrait of a Nazi soldier. "Albert Speer was Hitler's Minister of Armaments and War Production. After World War II, Speer was brought to trial. During his testimony, he said that he saw his role during the Holocaust as an administrator. And because he thought of himself as an administrator, he'd convinced himself that he didn't need to concern himself with matters regarding the treatment of human beings."

"He checked his humanity at the door," Taylor said.

"Wasn't he just doing his job?" Cory asked.

"That's what he told the courtroom," Palmer answered. "That he was just carrying out orders from his superiors. Philosopher and author Hannah Arendt calls this 'the banality of evil.'"

"I'm guessing that doesn't just happen in times of war?" Monty asked.

"It can happen in the workplace too," Palmer said. "Employees can separate their personal beliefs from the ethics of their workplace. After the subprime mortgage scandal in the early 2000s, for example, many people said they were just doing their jobs. They were acting in ways that they knew were clearly unethical, but they viewed their actions as permissible because they were acting on behalf of their employer or clients. They didn't question whether what they were doing was good for the individual, the community, or the common good."

"In any of those situations," Monty said, "it would have taken a lot of courage to speak up."

Edwin chimed in. "I'm not sure I would have pushed back if I were one of those engineers involved in the *Challenger* explosion."

"But why don't people act in these situations?" Monty asked.

Palmer smiled grimly. "You've arrived at the most terrifying aspect of all these events: the detachment people can show when observing events like the Holocaust."

Monty nodded. "Hitler wouldn't have been able to rise to power without the public's ambivalence."

"For evil to exist, sane, reasonable people must do nothing," Palmer added.

Palmer advanced the presentation to a portrait of a man leaning back in a wooden chair with a book open on his lap. "While Victor Frankl was imprisoned in a Nazi concentration camp, he took notes on napkins that later became his book *Man's Search for Meaning*."

The last photograph in the presentation was the unmistakable mushroom cloud of an exploding atomic bomb.

"Frankl said it best at the end of his book: 'So let us be alert—alert in a twofold sense. Since Auschwitz we know what man is capable of. And since Hiroshima we know what is at stake.'"

CHAPTER SIXTEEN

Monty walked into Sonja's office and noticed that she was on the phone. He carefully eased the large wooden door shut. Sonja gestured for Monty to sit in a chair in front of her desk, where her book, *The Empathy Gene*, was propped up and facing visitors.

"We're only halfway through the summer, Congressman," Sonja spoke into the phone. It takes more than a month and a half to change a teenager's moral constitution."

Monty scanned the office. A framed cover of *Time Magazine* hung on one wall. Sonja was featured on the cover, holding a red apple in front of her. The headline read *No More Bad Apples*, and beneath it ran the subtitle *Are the ethical an endangered species?*

On a nearby shelf, the book *Why I Left Goldman Sachs: A Wall Street Story* by Greg Smith caught Monty's eye. He remembered an interview in which Sonja had said the book had hit a nerve with her. It showed how a smart, ambitious Wall Street type like Smith helped bring the economy to its knees in the 2000s with reckless and criminal behavior. Beside the book, a plaque displayed a list of Woodward's donors. The largest investment, over a million dollars, was listed as coming from Anonymous.

As Sonja talked on the phone, she twisted her hair nervously. "Let's look at the results when classes end in August, Congressman. I think you will be pleased." There was a pause, and then she hung up the phone.

"I apologize, Mr. Hayward. It was inappropriate for you to hear that."

"Call me Monty," he insisted.

"Very well." Sonja tapped the screen on her phone, and music began playing throughout the room. "This piece is called *The Marriage of Figaro*. You like Mozart?"

"Sure, he's an up-and-comer." Monty grinned.

Sonja shook her head disapprovingly. "You and Edwin are quite the jokesters." She cleared her throat. "It didn't take long for you to get into trouble at the hospital. Dr. Sax told me about your stunt in the ambulance. Care to explain yourself?"

Monty shrugged. "Seemed like the right thing to do."

Sonja stood up and glared. "It was foolish, not to mention illegal. Give me one reason why I shouldn't send you home today."

Monty thought about that for a moment. "Because, instead of following the rules, I did the right thing—the human thing."

"I'm not sure whether what you did was wrong or right. A gray area, I suppose." Sonja shifted her gaze down to her desk and seemed temporarily transfixed by the music. "It took guts. Ironically, it took moral imagination."

She walked around her desk and past Monty,

motioning for him to follow her. They stepped out onto a balcony that hung about 30 feet above the ground for a panoramic view of the Atlantic Ocean. A lighthouse hugged the coastline. Farther offshore, a sailboat caught a gust of wind and tipped sideways.

"Tell me, Monty . . ." Sonja said, "How much imagination did it take to fake your way into Woodward Academy?"

Did she just say—

"Your father is all over the news, I'm sure you're aware. But anyone could have figured this out with a Google search."

Monty's heart started racing. "I'm confused," he said slowly.

"The day we reviewed applicants to Woodward, your father was giving a speech, and you and your mother were standing beside him."

"I don't know what you're talking about."

"You can cut the act, Mr. Hughes."

Monty sighed, knowing his cover was blown.

"I know you took your friend Joseph's identity. I've known since the first day. Do you know why I let you stay?"

Monty stared at Sonja blankly.

"First of all, if you graduate and do something special, it'll be good PR for the academy. What I found most interesting about you, though, is that you scored a negative on my test. Unlike your classmates, you actually *have* empathy. Considering your defibrillation stunt, you have a lot of it. And yet, you were desperate to get into my school."

"You offered a way to vaccinate me from becoming

someone like my father."

Sonja grinned. "I find your self-doubt, your preemptive guilt, compelling and worth exploring. I wonder if you're slowly realizing that maybe you're not so different from your dad, or any of the 'bad apples' you've been studying in class."

Not knowing how to respond to that, Monty stared out into the ocean.

"There's a lot of money in this school. Your actions at the hospital could have jeopardized what I'm trying to achieve. This is your warning, Monty."

"And what about this secret we now have?"

"Stay out of trouble, and we won't have a problem."

CHAPTER SEVENTEEN

It was a Saturday, and Monty ran along a coastal path with Taylor, Jonathan, and Edwin following behind. Monty sprinted ahead, positioning himself at the front of the group. The cool sea breeze pushed at his back as the other students trailed behind, laboring to keep pace.

"Congra . . . tulations," Edwin said, breathing heavily.

Monty turned his head to look back at Edwin. "For what?"

"For being . . . the first to get in . . . trouble with Sonja. I had my money . . . on Taylor."

Taylor coughed, out of breath. "I'm practically . . . Mother Teresa . . . compared to you. Why does three miles . . . feel like a marathon?"

"Gets you up from . . . your laptop," Edwin said.

Taylor smacked Edwin's hat off his head.

Coach Bode yelled through his loudspeaker from a motorboat near the shore. "Stop messing around. Stay on pace. I want eight-minute miles."

From the shore, Monty watched several crew boats

glide along behind Coach Bode's boat. Cory and Kirsten rowed a two-person boat; others controlled four- and eight-person boats. The bay was an ideal spot for rowing practice. It protected crew boats from wind and waves and allowed athletes to complete the rowing competition's average race distance of 1500 meters. Monty watched Cory and Kirsten propel their boat together, moving in unison, in sync. It was "swing," according to Coach Bode, and it was fun to watch.

Taylor stumbled over a rock, then regained her balance. "What'd you get in trouble over, anyway?" she asked Monty.

"Oh, you know, I pulled a fire alarm," Monty snickered.

Taylor shot Monty a sideways glance. "Had to be pretty serious if Dr. Woodward pulled you into her office."

It was clear to Monty that most of his classmates saw him as one of the more emotionally well students at Woodward, a goodie goodie, even. Monty had never thought of himself that way, though. Sure, he'd help an elderly person cross the street like any respectful citizen, and he'd advanced to Eagle Scout in the Boy Scouts of America, but he wasn't the perfect little angel that everyone was making him out to be.

At The Goldman School, Monty had cheated on tests like most of his classmates. He and Joseph would throw snowballs at cars in their neighborhood and run away laughing. Once, on a dare from Joseph, Monty knocked a neighbor's mailbox off its post with a baseball bat, an incident that cost him a visit to the local police station. In Monty's mind, these were the juvenile actions of an adolescent boy. They were a far cry from Edwin's plagiarism, Cory's SAT cheating scandal, and Taylor's computer hacking. They were *nothing* like the criminal acts his father had committed. At Woodward, Monty hoped to avoid the possibility of escalation.

Palmer had introduced the students to a sociological theory known as the "broken windows theory." According to the theory, if someone gets away with a small infraction, they're more likely to escalate and commit a more serious infraction in the future. For instance, if someone were to throw a rock at a house, break a window, and isn't caught, they're more likely to do something more serious later on. They could perhaps break into a house, perhaps even steal. The broken windows theory states that if this person is caught at the stage of the 'broken window,' they're less likely to escalate, having felt that their actions have consequences.

"What's Sonja like?" Jonathan asked.

Monty thought about that for a moment. Sonja was stoic, high-powered, difficult to read. She was also philosophical, perceptive, and uncomfortably self-aware. "She's complex."

"Well, while you're getting into trouble in your internship, I'm building a rad video game with a game designer on the island," Taylor said.

"I just got my first assignment from Amy Baker," Edwin told the group.

"What are you working on?" Monty asked.

"We're looking into this Richard Hughes guy."

If Edwin went digging around in his father's life, Monty thought, he might discover who he really was.

Just then, a pack of runners passed Monty and the others at a blistering pace. Their T-shirts read *Nantucket Rowing Club*.

The student whose shirt said *Captain* had dark hair and an athletic build. Monty gritted his teeth and skipped into a sprint. The captain noticed Monty over his shoulder and sped up, but Monty accelerated to keep pace. The boy's pace quickened again, and so did Monty's. There was a lighthouse a few hundred feet away, and the captain squinted at it. Understanding it was their finish line, Monty broke into a full sprint, passing the captain.

A hundred feet from the lighthouse, Palmer appeared alongside the running path. He had his head titled back, lost in thought. Monty tried to pivot, but he smashed into his teacher, and they both tumbled into the sand.

Monty pushed himself to his feet quickly. He wiped sand from his face and watched the other team's captain climb the steps of the lighthouse triumphantly. He raised a fist into the air and smiled smugly at Monty. Monty shook his head and turned to see Palmer wincing in pain. He took his teacher's hand and lifted him to his feet.

"I'm really sorry about that, Dr. Reid," Monty said.

Palmer knocked sand off the front of his pants. "That's all right, Monty. I was just taking my daily walk. I should have seen you."

By then, the other team and the Woodward kids had reached the lighthouse. Monty walked with Palmer. He'd seen his teacher take his walks. The same time, every day. "What do you think about during your walks?"

"I dwell on ideas. Sit with uncomfortable emotions. Face them, rather than ignore them. Afterward, they have less of a hold on me. A lot of times, I try not to think at all. If a thought comes, I notice it, then let it go."

As Palmer led Monty to the dock, Monty asked, "Where are you going?"

"I'm doing repairs on my boat today."

"Seems like you've made a lot of progress since I last saw it. Can I come see it?"

"Of course," Palmer replied.

Palmer led Monty onto the boat and below deck to a small living room, ducking as he entered. "It's fully livable now. A working kitchen, head, heat, and electricity."

He pulled a frying pan from a cabinet. "You want anything to eat? I was going to make an egg sandwich. The best in New England."

"That would be great, thanks."

Monty took in their surroundings while Palmer retrieved ingredients from the refrigerator. Palmer broke two eggs into the frying pan, which sizzled. He noticed Monty examining the diplomas on the walls.

"All that schooling, and still no one wants to listen to me," Palmer said.

Monty chuckled. "Why is that?"

"Most of us are quite happy living with our illusions. Most people react negatively, in some cases with hostility, to the truth-teller who examines paradoxes, points out inconsistencies, and shatters those illusions."

Monty lifted his chin toward a poster of Albert Einstein. The photograph showed the physicist playfully sticking out his tongue. "Einstein loved to sail, right?"

"It's where he did a lot of his thought experiments," Palmer replied. "Sailing gave him the peace of mind to think freely about physics and the cosmos."

Palmer flipped a fried egg and tapped the pan with the spatula. "I was very interested in what you wrote in your essay. It was fine writing, Monty. You wrote about the scientist in the news who committed fraud." Palmer set a breakfast sandwich onto the table.

Monty began eating, avoiding contact with Palmer.

"I'm sure you know that if you put a frog in boiling water, it'll jump out," Palmer said, "but if you place a frog in cool water and gradually turn up the heat, the frog will boil to death. Perhaps it was the same way with this scientist. Perhaps he lost his ethical footing, very slowly."

Palmer set down the essay Monty had written in class—the one he had thrown in the trash. Palmer walked to the kitchen and continued cooking.

Monty reread his own words. The soul-crushing realization that his father and role model was a liar and a criminal. Rereading his essay, he realized that he hadn't gradually lost respect for his father. When he learned about the fraud, he'd lost respect in one moment. "And here I am," he had written, "trying to make sense of the shame while he falls from grace. What do his actions say about me? My tendencies? My future? He's my father, my blood. What does that make me capable of?"

Monty looked up from the paper and locked eyes with Palmer. He waited for Palmer to accuse him of lying his way onto the island, as Sonja had. But Palmer only nodded imperceptibly. Monty was relieved.

"I know it must feel like you're doomed, in a way," Palmer said. "Because of where you came from."

"Because of *who* I came from."

Palmer shrugged. "Do you feel responsible for the fraud?"

"I do."

"Did you know your father was committing fraud?"

"Does it matter?"

Palmer sat across from Monty at the table and took a

bite from an egg sandwich.

"What do you want, Monty?" Palmer asked.

"I don't know." Monty shook his head. "I really don't know."

"It's okay not to have answers." Palmer knocked on the wooden table. "My favorite philosopher was Immanuel Kant, who said, 'Out of the crooked timber of humanity, no straight thing was ever made.'"

Monty laughed. "So, we're all made from crooked timber?"

Palmer nodded. "We all have flaws, imperfections, and weaknesses built into the fabric of who we are. Character is the struggle against our weaknesses."

"But those flaws cause so much trouble in the world. We make mistakes, we hurt people, sometimes by accident."

"We do, but we also have the capacity to recognize our harmful actions. We can feel ashamed and overcome them. This is the struggle we have with ourselves."

Palmer grabbed a notebook off the table. "I want you to go to the library and get this book." On the first page of the notebook, he wrote down *The Drama of the Gifted Child: The Search for the True Self* by Alice Miller. Then he pushed the notebook toward Monty.

"Start to think in these terms: not what *you* want from life, but rather what *life* wants from you. As you read and think, write down your thoughts in this notebook. Write freely; don't self-edit. Write about your family. Write about your father. Write about memories that seem difficult to bear. Let your curiosity be stronger than your fear."

Monty stared at the notebook for a moment and then

looked at Palmer's bookshelf. It held a whole row of notebooks, presumably the result of Palmer doing just what he was preaching. Monty set down his sandwich and turned back to Palmer. "Why?"

"Because this is how we find out what we want. What we fear. Who we are."

At Nantucket Cottage Hospital, Monty only had 15 minutes before he needed to join the other interns for rounds in the intensive care unit with Dr. Sax. He'd just stopped into the hospital's cafeteria when he saw Laura reading quietly at a table.

She was bringing the straw of an iced coffee to her lips when Monty caught her eye. As she set the cup on the table, it tipped, and coffee spilled across her book. Hurrying closer, Monty swiped some paper napkins from a dispenser and handed them to her.

Laura dabbed the book with the napkins. "I'm such a klutz."

Monty sat in the seat across from her and pointed to her notebook. "How are the poems coming along?"

Laura indicated her book with the now-damp napkins: *Moby Dick*. "I can't stop reading long enough to start writing."

"*Moby Dick*'s a classic," Monty said. "I don't blame you."

"It's wonderful imagining how Nantucket used to be."

Monty shifted in his seat, pausing to gather his thoughts. "I wanted to apologize for what I did in the ambulance. It was impulsive. Reckless."

Laura looked taken aback. "Please don't feel bad. You did what you thought was right." She finished cleaning the book. "I've always looked up to my grandmother. She's strong and independent, and she loved my grandfather."

"What was it like to learn she had a DNR?"

"When my grandfather passed, she lost the fight in her. I didn't come to Nantucket this summer to prolong her life; I came to provide comfort in her final days."

Monty was listening, his head slightly tilted.

Laura took a sip of her iced coffee and examined him.

"Why are you looking at me like that?" he asked.

"You just don't seem like the kind of kid who should be at Woodward."

"How did you know I was attending Woodward?"

"It's a small island," she said with a smile. "Anyway, the news makes it seem like no one there can feel anything."

Monty shrugged. "I'm different, I guess."

"In a good way." Laura smiled, then tossed the ball of used napkins into a nearby trash can. "So, my uncle works at Moralis. He can't tell me much, but he says their scientists are experimenting with some gene-editing technologies."

Monty shrugged. "I'm not sure about Dr. Woodward and her lab yet, honestly. I think she's at least trying to improve things."

"I would keep your eyes open."

"I will."

CHAPTER EIGHTEEN

For Monty, the summer days were all starting to blur together. The classes, homework, internship at the hospital, and jogs around the island with the crew team had taken over his life. His arms, legs, and back were firm from rowing and lifting weights, and he could run at least seven-minute miles.

Monty had been reading *The Drama of the Gifted Child*. As he read, he recorded his thoughts in a journal. Despite setting athletic records in school, achieving near-perfect grades, and being accepted into Ivy League universities, Monty had never felt like "enough," especially for his father. Miller's book argued that such feelings of emptiness and alienation were paradoxically common among high achievers like himself. They resulted from a child's desperate search for a parent's love and approval.

Palmer's lessons on morality were starting to sink in with the students. For today's class, he wrote *moral muteness* on the whiteboard, then turned to address the class. "Who knows what this means?"

Monty answered, having done the reading the night before. "When you see something wrong but look the other way."

Palmer nodded. "Less than fifty percent of people who witness unethical behavior within an organization will report it. Why do you think that is?"

"Most people don't want to stick their neck out," Monty said.

"Because they're afraid it'll get cut off," Edwin added.

Palmer smiled. "A fascinating study performed by a psychologist named Harold Takooshian demonstrated this point beautifully. Takooshian and his team put fur coats, cameras, and televisions into locked cars around New York City and then sent a team of volunteers to break into the cars and steal the merchandise. The volunteers were instructed to make their thefts as conspicuous as possible, so onlookers would notice. Of the about eight thousand people who witnessed a break-in, about seven thousand didn't even notice. But how many people do you think tried to stop them?"

"Six hundred?" Cory guessed.

"Less than that," Taylor shot back. "A couple hundred, I bet."

"About a dozen people tried to stop the break-ins," Palmer said.

Later that day, Palmer and the students met at Moralis. Every time Monty entered Moralis and saw scientists working at lab benches, he was reminded of his science internship at Nautilus. In high school, Monty had thought lab work was dull. Other students seemed to relish the opportunity to carry out experiments with their hands, solving puzzles with their minds. He was less interested in the lab but more interested in the clinic. In fact, every encounter with the reality of basic research was just another reminder that he had the soul of a doctor, not a scientist.

Edwin walked in step with Palmer. "What are we learning this hour, Teach?"

"The proper method for applying duct tape to your mouth?" Taylor guessed.

The other students laughed while Edwin unsuccessfully searched for a comeback.

Palmer used his badge to open a door. "Today, we're going to watch a reenactment of the Stanley Milgram experiment from 1961. In the study, subjects were broken into two groups–students and teachers–and then separated into two rooms."

Sonja appeared in the hallway with Mr. Aldrich by her side. "Dr. Reid, could I have a word, please?"

"Of course," Palmer said.

Mr. Aldrich stayed behind, watching the students. Palmer and Sonja walked down the hallway and out of earshot. Palmer nodded his head while Sonja spoke quietly. The conversation ended, and Palmer and Sonja walked back.

"Monty, I want you to go with Dr. Woodward," Palmer said. "Edwin, please go with Mr. Aldrich."

Monty and Edwin looked at each other, unsure of what was happening, but they complied. Sonja and Mr. Aldrich led the boys down the hallway and disappeared into rooms.

"Well, that was weird," Jonathan said.

"Are they going to have their kidneys when we see them again?" Kirsten asked.

Palmer raised his hands to calm the students. "They'll be fine, guys. Dr. Woodward thought it would be best to have students participate in this live experiment."

"Only a matter of time before we became Woodward's guinea pigs," Taylor said.

Ignoring the comment, Palmer led the students into a small room. There was a table set against one wall. Above it was a window, perhaps ten feet wide and six feet in height, which looked out onto two other similarly sized rooms.

"A two-way mirror," Cory said, pressing a hand against the glass.

Taylor stuck her tongue out at the glass. "We can see them, but they can't see us."

Palmer nodded. "They can't hear us either."

There was a table in the center of the room to the left. On the table was a microphone and a dial labeled from "75 volts" to "450 volts," increasing by increments of twenty-five.

"In this experiment," Palmer explained, "Monty will play the 'teacher' in the room on the left; he will ask Edwin, the 'student,' in the room on the right, questions through the microphone. If Edwin answers a question incorrectly, Monty will be instructed by a doctor to administer an electric shock. These shocks become increasingly stronger with each wrong answer from the student. Now, it's important to note that Edwin, the student, is part of the study. The shocks aren't real, and he has been instructed to fake reactions to the electricity."

"This should be interesting," Jonathan said, leaning close to the mirror.

The door to the room on the left opened and Jessica walked in. She was wearing an ivory-colored physician's coat—clearly the experimenter—and directed Monty to take a seat at the table. He was the "teacher." The door of the room on the right opened, and Edwin sat down. The "student." A technician powered on his laptop and then began attaching wires to Edwin's skin.

Palmer asked the students, "Have you ever wanted to please an authority figure so much that it clouded your judgment?"

"Before we came here, we had to submit proof of our vaccinations," Cory said. "I've had them all—hepatitis B and others. My mom had all the documentation to prove it, except for tuberculosis."

"You forged it?" Kirsten asked.

Cory shrugged. "My mom said no one would notice or care."

"Obedience," Palmer said. "A teacher, parent, boss, even a religious leader can cloud our ethical judgment, especially when we want them to like us."

Palmer continued to narrate the experiment as the students huddled around the glass. "Again, Monty is the teacher; Dr. Woodward has told him that he's participating in an experiment that's testing learning and memory in adults."

In the other room, Jessica was explaining the "experiment" to Monty, sitting at the table.

Palmer continued. "Jessica is playing the role of the experimenter. She's explaining the study's premise: a test of Edwin's memory. Remember, Jessica and Edwin are in on the experiment. Edwin will be pretending. The only real subject is Monty."

In the other room, Jessica lowered her clipboard and explained the experiment. "Many theories help explain how people learn. In this experiment, Monty, you are playing the role of the teacher. Edwin in the other room is playing the role of the student." She pointed to the device on the table. "The red button on that device delivers an electric shock to Edwin."

Monty examined the device cautiously.

"Through this microphone, you will be testing Edwin's ability to recall accurately sets of word pairs," Jessica continued. "For example, you may ask Edwin to remember the following pairs: *microwave-telephone*, *mountain-skyscraper*, *entrepreneurial-stream*. If Edwin inaccurately recalls the word pair, you will deliver a shock."

Monty's eyebrows rose. "What kind of shock are we talking about here?"

"The shocks begin at seventy-five volts, about as painful as a mosquito bite. I will increase the voltage with each mistake."

On the other side of the mirror, Palmer said, "Now, remember, Jessica and Edwin are pretending. Edwin will deliberately answer questions incorrectly. Jessica is there to urge Monty to continue the experiment, despite any resistance. The point of the experiment is to see how long Monty will continue to deliver shocks, even when he knows they're causing pain to Edwin."

"There's no way Monty will go to the max voltage," Kirsten said.

"Let's begin," Jessica told Monty.

Monty read the first set of word pairs. Right on cue,

Edwin recited the word pairs back incorrectly. Monty glanced at Jessica, who nodded. Monty pressed the button and delivered a shock. Through the speakers, they could hear Edwin grunt in discomfort.

"Edwin's faking, right?" Taylor asked.

Palmer nodded.

The experiment continued through several more rounds. With each, the "shocks" became more powerful.

Looking uneasy, Monty asked Jessica, "Are you sure this isn't hurting Edwin?"

Jessica was stone-faced. "Please continue the experiment."

Monty continued. Again, Edwin failed. Again, another shock, this time 200 volts. Edwin shouted through the speakers.

Monty's leg bounced nervously. He drummed his fingers on the table.

The shocks progressed to two hundred seventy-five. Then three hundred. Then three hundred twenty-five. Such shocks wouldn't have been lethal, of course, but they would hurt like hell.

"I don't think I can do this," Monty said. "This doesn't feel right."

Jessica prodded him. "It's important that you continue the experiment." She gestured toward the microphone.

Monty ran a hand through his hair. "What if something happens to him?"

Jessica didn't react. She only glanced at the microphone, urging Monty to continue.

Another wrong answer. Another shock.

Edwin began crying softly through the speakers. "I'm done with this," he yelled. "Get me out of here! I have anxiety, you know. I think I'm having a panic attack!"

Monty looked horrified. "He wants to stop. He says he's panicking."

Jessica delivered the same unenthusiastic response: The experiment must continue. Monty stared at the table. He shook his head and turned the dial to the next shock. Four hundred fifty volts. A final incorrect response.

Edwin howled in agony.

Palmer turned to the students. "What can we learn from this experiment?"

"That people are monsters," Cory responded.

"Sadists, more specifically," Taylor added.

The door to the room opened, and Jessica led Monty and Edwin into the room.

Monty looked Edwin up and down, and said, "Are you okay, man? I feel horrible."

"Monty, you were part of an experiment," Palmer said. "Everyone was in on it, except for you."

Monty glanced at Palmer and then back at Edwin. "You were faking it?"

Edwin made a fake gun with his hand. "Gotcha!"

Monty examined Palmer's face. "You tricked me?"

"I'm sorry if you feel that you were deceived, Monty, but the experiment showed us that people can disregard their consciences in the presence of an authority figure." Palmer pointed at Jessica's white coat. "We are especially vulnerable when these authority figures are wearing special clothes or uniforms. Physicians, police officers, even a boss in a three-piece suit."

"But most people wouldn't get to the highest voltage, right?" Monty asked.

"Before Milgram started his experiment," Palmer said,

"he asked leading psychologists to predict what percentage of teachers might advance to four hundred and fifty volts. They concluded that only a sadistic person would get to four hundred fifty volts and cause that much pain in another person."

"What percentage of the population are actually sadists?" Jonathan asked.

"About one percent," Palmer said. "That's why the psychologists predicted that only one percent of the teachers would reach the final voltage."

"What did the results show?" Monty asked.

"Two-thirds of the teachers reached the highest voltage."

"Like I said," Jonathan spoke up. "We're all monsters."

"Or rather, given the right circumstances, we're all capable of doing something monstrous," Palmer corrected.

"If Monty went to the highest voltage," Edwin said, "then all of us are screwed."

CHAPTER NINETEEN

At the front of Palmer's classroom stood a handsome forty-something man in a stylish suit. To look at him, Monty wouldn't have guessed he was a convicted felon. He could have passed for any of his father's high-powered business associates; he could have given the keynote address at a charity fundraiser.

Palmer had told the students that Wayne Price was visiting, so Monty had looked him up online before class. He learned that the former lobbyist had served eight years in prison for white-collar crimes, including tax fraud and money laundering.

"Class, I would like you to welcome Mr. Price," Palmer told the students. He turned to Wayne and forced a smile. "This summer, we've talked about various organizational and psychological pressures that can cause otherwise well-intentioned people to ignore their consciences. For better or worse, Wayne has firsthand experience in these matters, and he was gracious enough to come visit us to talk about it."

Wayne cleared his throat and used the remote control in his hand to project an image of the McDowell Federal Correctional Institution onto the large screen behind him. Despite his incarceration, with his all-American looks, tailored suit, and occasional Cheshire Cat grin, Wayne clearly thought he was still a master of the universe.

"For eight years, this was my home. I lived with drug dealers, murderers, rapists—the hardest criminals on the planet. It was a dangerous place, and I constantly worried for my safety."

Wayne advanced the presentation to an image of a prison cell so small, it barely accommodated a sink and toilet. The bed was a concrete slab without blankets or a pillow.

"This is solitary confinement, otherwise known as 'the hole.' The prison staff would isolate me here to prevent beatings from other inmates. I ate and slept here for twenty-two hours a day, sometimes for months at a time, without human contact."

The next image showed a ten-foot-wide courtyard with a concrete floor and brick walls rising maybe 30 feet toward the sky. A patch of light filtered through a tiny window in the ceiling. "This unfortunate-looking concrete playground was where I was allowed thirty minutes of 'recreation' each day."

Wayne paused before he advanced the slide to an image of him with a pregnant woman. "I wasn't there when my son was born. I destroyed my marriage. I lost the career I loved. And of course, I lost my freedom."

"Sounds a lot like Woodward," Edwin blurted out.

The class erupted in laughter.

Palmer narrowed his gaze. "Tell us what you did for work, Wayne."

"I ran the most successful lobbying firm in Washington, DC."

"So what happened?" Kirsten asked.

"All I cared about was winning for my clients. Over the years, I stopped caring about how I got those wins. I bribed politicians, lawmakers, and regulators. I took kickbacks and evaded taxes. I bent the rules, then I broke them."

"Can you tell us how you managed psychologically while you were breaking these laws?" Palmer asked.

Wayne raised two fingers. "Two words: *creative rationalization.* See, I cared deeply about my clients' issues. I solved important problems for them; I protected and advanced their interests. I helped them shape laws and saved them millions of dollars, in some cases. But I stopped caring about the means I used to solve their problems. I stopped caring about where the line was drawn in the sand."

Out of the corner of his eye, Monty saw Edwin typing something into his phone. He scrolled through a list of search results until a picture of Wayne appeared on the screen. Edwin caught Monty's eye and zoomed in on one paragraph of the article, holding the phone so Monty could read it.

After serving eight years in prison, Wayne now crisscrosses the country on a speaking tour, giving lessons to young adults, showing them the error of his ways. Another picture embedded in the article showed Wayne eating breakfast at a table in a diner. *Due to modest sales from his book and speaking events, Wayne also consults as an accountant. One client of his is The Greasy Spoon Diner in Waltham, Massachusetts.*

On his other side, Edwin whispered something in

Taylor's ear and showed her the same article. She laughed, then discretely slid her phone from her pocket and began typing with a grin.

Oblivious, Palmer asked Wayne, "Weren't some of the practices you participated in part of the culture in Washington?"

"Everyone was doing these sketchy deals. So many people were bribing politicians, taking kickbacks, and evading taxes. I was just the best at it. I was playing with the largest sums of money. My motto was, 'If you can do it, overdo it.'"

"But you knew you were breaking rules?" Kirsten asked.

"Breaking *laws*," Jonathan added.

Wayne nodded. "I chose causes I believed in. I thought I was helping people. I deluded myself into thinking I was doing good. I even donated money to organizations I thought were making positive changes in the world."

Taylor was busy on her smartphone. The screen was black, with green lines of code running horizontally. She was hacking, Monty thought, but what? He noticed a request for a username and password pop up on her screen. That's when he realized she was hacking Wayne's computer, most likely to control his presentation.

Taylor grinned when she caught Monty looking and raised a finger to her lips. Whatever she was up to, Wayne wasn't going to like it.

Wayne advanced his presentation to the image of a book that had his portrait on the cover. "I wrote this book to prevent others from making the same mistakes."

Apparently wrapping up his presentation, Wayne said, "Now I would like to thank you all for—"

The class exploded with laughter.

There was an altered image of Wayne at The Greasy Spoon Diner projected onto the screen. It showed him wearing an oversized chef's hat and an apron and holding a wooden ladle.

Wayne's face turned red. Obviously trying to keep his cool, he said, "Okay, very funny, guys." He turned to Palmer. "These kids are clever, huh?"

Palmer shrugged, looking a bit amused himself.

Wayne raised a finger and tilted it toward the now-raucous class, delivering his final lesson. "Clever is good, but make sure you use that intelligence to color within the lines."

Palmer raised a hand, and the students quieted down.

"I was the picture of the American dream, in charge of my own life," Wayne continued when the class was listening again. "Now, I have to write 'felon' on every job application I ever fill out. I can't vote. I can't own a firearm. I lost everything." He paused. "Under the wrong circumstances, you might be surprised by what you are capable of. Just remember: You came to Woodward to avoid ending up like me."

As Monty walked back to his dorm room, he thought about Wayne. Initially, he'd been repulsed by the man's greed and unchecked ambition. His willingness to break rules, skirt laws, and cut corners if it would help achieve his clients' goals. Monty realized that Wayne seemed a lot like his father. They had similar mindsets in that the ends always seemed to justify the means. Wasn't it this flawed thinking that led to both of their demises?

On the other hand, listening to Wayne explain why he'd done what he'd done had allowed Monty to see his father through a different lens. Ever since Monty had learned about Richard's fraud, he'd defined himself as everything his father was *not*. Not ethical. Not honest. *Not a good man*. But having learned more about Wayne, Monty realized there were more dimensions to his father's crimes.

In that moment, Monty wasn't as repulsed by his father. Could he even sympathize with him? Richard had wanted to provide for and protect his family. He must've been under so much pressure to succeed. Monty thought about how lonely his father must have felt while keeping that big secret for so many years. Monty even wondered what he might have done if he'd been in similar circumstances with a business to lead and a family to protect.

CHAPTER TWENTY

When Palmer walked into Sonja's office, she was pedaling vigorously on a stationary bike, facing a large mirror. She sipped from a water bottle as she met Palmer's eyes in the mirror. "How are classes going?"

Sonja seemed to have become more high-strung during their weekly updates. The money the government had infused into the school was not without strings. With only a month left in the summer, Congress had grown impatient, requesting reports with tangible results and fewer promises.

"A mentor of mine once said that teaching consists of pounding abstract ideas into concrete skulls," Palmer said.

Sonja slapped a hand against the bike's handlebars. "Give it to me straight, Dr. Reid."

"Most students are responding. They're making connections, gaining insight."

"Any standouts?" Sonja wiped sweat from her face with her hand and continued pedaling.

"Monty is motivated," Palmer said. "Eager, as if he

were cramming for an exam."

Sonja stood up on the pedals and worked them faster, but she was barely out of breath. "Did you hear about the incident at the hospital?"

Palmer grabbed a towel from the back of Sonja's chair and handed it to her. "I thought it took courage to resuscitate that woman in the ambulance."

Sonja threw her towel over a shoulder. "Anyone falling behind in class?"

Palmer was hesitant to identify any *nonresponders*, as Sonja had referred to them in the Academy's business plan. Palmer knew that students moved at their own pace, and it was too early to tell if Edwin—if any students for that matter—could be helped at Woodward. Certainly, it was too early to deploy CRISPR treatment. He hoped it never came to that.

Sonja stepped off the bike and folded one leg up behind her for a stretch. "Other teachers say Edwin has acted out repeatedly. Do you have any thoughts on that?"

"I see that as a good sign, actually."

Sonja pulled back the other leg. "How's that?"

"Humor serves an important psychological function. For Freud, humor was a way to tell the truth while also concealing the truth, a pro-social way to express aggression—"

Sonja raised a hand to dismiss Palmer's psychobabble, as she was prone to calling it. Palmer had begun to relish the opportunities to fire Sonja up with his psychological knowledge. It was like theater.

"There was another incident during Wayne's presentation?"

"A practical joke, really."

"I had hoped Wayne would have a positive experience during his visit. He's on a book tour right now. Who knows what he will say about Woodward when he goes on the morning news."

"It was Taylor who hacked the man's presentation," Palmer pointed out.

"But Edwin engineered the stunt."

"Wayne is a felon," Palmer said. "He must know that people aren't going to treat him like royalty wherever he goes."

Sonja straightened from her stretches and ran her fingers over a globe on her desk. Then with a flick of her wrist, she set the globe spinning. "I discussed the incident with Mr. and Mrs. Thompson."

"Again, 'incident' is a strong word, Sonja."

"Nevertheless, Edwin's parents were disturbed. They won't have another scandal. We discussed taking more aggressive measures."

"Oh?"

"It's clear that Edwin isn't responding to your teachings."

"He just needs more time," Palmer pleaded. "These students don't just need knowledge of moral principles; they need someone to address the root causes of their problems."

"Oh please," Sonja scoffed. "These rich kids probably had idyllic childhoods."

"Sure, they may not have have had to worry about whether they had enough food, water, or shelter. They might've had access to the best schools and resources, but that doesn't mean they don't have problems. They have too many choices in terms of careers or where they could go to school or live with no idea how to choose. They're under overwhelming pressure to excel. Many experience mood disorders, like anxiety or depression, in epic proportions."

"Are you referring to anyone in particular?"

"Monty, for one. He comes from wealth, but he's clearly struggling. Running from something, or someone. It's not uncommon for high-achieving, 'gifted' young adults like Monty to feel a sense of alienation or emptiness. Kids like him sometimes use their talents and special abilities as a way to win the love and respect they didn't get from their parents. I'm trying to address that emptiness. Until I do, he'll be lost."

Sonja walked across the room. "I will trust you with regard to Monty. As for Edwin, I disagree; his problems are not associated with his upbringing. His parents seem like good, caring people. Edwin's problems are biological. Nature, not nurture."

"Are you suggesting that someone like Edwin can't escape his genetic predisposition toward bad behavior? Doesn't that strike at the very core of what this school was designed to prevent?"

"I don't say this in interviews, Palmer, but I believe some people are born bad. We have proven in the lab that deficits in certain brain regions can lead to a lack of empathy—"

"Sonja, it's both nature *and* nurture. You said that in your interview with Amy. It's never just one. You're suggesting that someone like Hitler was born 'evil'?"

"Of course."

"And yet, look at the horrors of that man's childhood," Palmer implored. "His father constantly humiliated him, destroyed his sense of self-worth. I tell students here not to judge but to *understand*. The kids here are learning principles of honesty, respect, trust, and compassion, but I'm also creating a safe space for them to work through their complicated pasts."

Sonja stared at the plaque above her desk. The words *Beati Mundo Corde* were written on it: "Blessed are the pure in heart."

"Apparently," she said slowly, "I need to remind you why I built this school, Dr. Reid." She looked toward the window. "Out there, the situation is dire. Widespread corruption. The lying, cheating, and backstabbing. A sickening obsession with celebrity, fame, and wealth. This is the age of amorality. The age of decadence. Our country is under siege from a virus, Palmer. Woodward Academy is the vaccine. We are fighting this battle in the trenches. We are on the precipice of an ethical revolution. We will spark a golden age for morality. I don't care how timeouts made these kids feel when they were toddlers. I'm here to prevent them from operating within society like a wrecking ball."

"Are you going to use the CRISPR treatment on Edwin?" Palmer knew the answer; he just hoped it wouldn't be his hand on the lever.

"The Thompsons have already given me permission. And since you're the only psychiatrist at Woodward, you will administer the treatment."

"And what if I don't feel comfortable doing that?"

"Then you can sail your little boat back to Boston."

Palmer left Sonja's office, his head swimming. He sat on a stone seat in the middle of the school's courtyard and stared into the fountain. Black flies buzzed along the surface of the bubbling water. The nearby ocean lent the courtyard an air of peace, and Palmer often came here to think.

Was he really going to deliver the treatment to Edwin? Sonja's gene-editing tool was experimental and hadn't yet been evaluated by clinical trials. She and other scientists at Moralis barely knew how it changed the behaviors of animals, much less how it functioned in teenagers.

At the beginning of the summer, Sonja had told Palmer that her treatment had lowered aggression in rats, making them more docile. While they hadn't published their findings, Sonja and others at Moralis theorized that the activation of various genes associated with empathy reduced the rodents' aggression by lowering their stress response to fear. It was almost as if the animals had been domesticated, but the mechanism through which it occurred was still unknown.

Palmer watched scientists stroll the grounds, discussing ideas. They were simply doing Sonja's bidding, he thought, giving no thought to the possible unintended consequences of using CRISPR to activate "empathy" genes. These scientists—always asking, "What if we could...?" and never considering, "But should we?"

Why did it always take a philosopher to raise these questions? To sound the alarm?

Perhaps Sonja was right, though. Who knew if Woodward's curriculum really worked. Could exposing adolescents to ethical experiments, the science of morality and ancient wisdom overrule their biology? None of the teachings had been proven, after all. If Congress knew how little they actually knew, they would pull funding right away.

Palmer scanned the courtyard and saw some of his students enjoying themselves. Cory walked toward the gym, holding a protein shake in his hand. Kirsten was sitting on the beach, sketching in her notebook. Jonathan was sitting with his back against a tree while staring at his laptop, likely trading options.

Out of the corner of his eye, Palmer saw Monty and Edwin leaving the cafeteria together.

Playfully, Monty gripped his lower back. "Hey, man, my back's been killing me lately."

"Oh, yeah, why's that?" Edwin asked.

Monty socked Edwin in the arm. "Because I have to carry your sorry ass every time we row."

Edwin threw his head back and laughed. "Give me a break! We all know who our boat's MVP is."

Palmer smiled, pleased to see Monty laughing. When Monty had arrived at Woodward, he'd been somber, often serious, but the young man's burden appeared to have lifted somewhat. He smiled more, played more. It was a sign of progress, Palmer thought, an indication that his father was loosening its grip on the young man's psyche.

"Gentlemen," Palmer greeted them as they approached the fountain.

"Hey, Teach . . ." Edwin grinned sheepishly. "Sorry about Wayne's presentation yesterday. I just couldn't help myself."

Palmer raised a hand. "What's done is done, Mr. Thompson. I appreciate your apology, though."

Edwin spotted Taylor leaving the cafeteria. "Hey, Tay!

Video games, your place?"

"Dorms in five!" Taylor shouted back.

"You coming?" Edwin asked Monty.

Monty looked at Palmer, and Palmer gestured for Monty to sit on the stone seat.

"Suit yourself," Edwin said, running off to meet Taylor.

Palmer looked into the fountain. "What did you think of Wayne?"

"I was surprised, actually. I thought he'd be some hardened criminal. Antisocial and aggressive, or something. But he seemed smart and reflective. A nice guy. A *normal* guy."

Palmer's thoughts drifted for a moment, his eyes focusing on the bubbling water. He still couldn't shake his meeting with Sonja.

"Something wrong?" Monty asked.

Palmer gazed up at Sonja's balcony. "Woodward . . ."

Monty narrowed his eyes.

Palmer shook his head and finished his thought. "I just don't know if my teachings, or this school, are helping."

"But we've learned so much from you, Dr. Reid. You've shared cautionary tales. Shown us pitfalls to avoid, common traps that people can fall into if they're not careful. I've found it valuable."

"I'm glad you think so, Monty, but not everyone feels that way."

"Like who?"

Palmer thought of Sonja and her order to deliver the treatment. It was bigger than her, though. Could they keep these future outlaws out of trouble by explaining how the Holocaust had happened or why the Challenger had exploded or by showing them what people were capable of by reenacting the Stanley Milgram experiment? Palmer couldn't be sure. Woodward Academy was an experiment, after all.

"I'm actually not on sabbatical from The Hastings Center," Palmer confessed. "Before I came to Woodward, I resigned from my academic position."

"Why'd you do that?"

"Let me tell you a story, Monty." Palmer took a deep breath. "In 1926, Charles Eliot died at the age of ninety-two. He was Harvard's longest-serving president. Reporters across the country worked on articles about Eliot's extraordinary career and life. The man had an enormous impact on the world as an educator, scientist, and writer. His thoughts helped shape our country's intellectual, cultural, and moral life."

A small bird flew down and perched on the edge of the fountain. Palmer studied the bird for a moment before continuing. "But the day after Eliot's death, the famous silent film actor Rudolph Valentino passed away. The coverage was all over the radio and newspapers. It was nonstop. With shocking speed, everyone forgot about Eliot."

"We admire entertainers more than our educators," Monty said.

Palmer nodded. "For me, that marked the end of our country's reverence for traditional leaders and started our love affair with celebrities. We value the young and beautiful more than the old and wise. By coming here, I thought I could help get our priorities straight. More than ever, our kids need *heroes*, not celebrities. They're hungry for real leadership."

"You're a leader, Dr. Reid."

Palmer thought about what Sonja had asked him to do—how he hadn't mustered the guts to tell her he wouldn't deliver the treatment. "I think you're a real leader, Monty."

Monty looked taken aback.

Palmer could see that Monty, despite looking better, was still wounded, still fighting his demons. Palmer rested a hand on Monty's shoulder. "Sometimes we see things in other people before we see them in ourselves."

Palmer realized that Monty had started to idealize him—and that wasn't necessarily a good thing. The problem with idealization was that Monty was putting Palmer on a pedestal without acknowledging the negative aspects of his teacher's character. Monty was denying the real possibility—the truth, in fact—that Palmer, while principled, was just as susceptible to the same psychological and organizational forces that he'd been teaching in the classroom.

Monty was smart, though. Palmer knew he'd learn that idealizing someone was a denial of reality. With time, Monty would accept that every human is complex, even flawed. Palmer hoped that Monty would then replace his idealization with admiration. He hoped Monty could admire his teacher's positive qualities while accepting his negative, all-too human ones. He hoped he could help Monty realize that even philosophers had trouble finding the courage to do the right thing. Helping Monty realize this truth would be Palmer's greatest lesson.

A few hours later, Palmer was leading the students up a coastal path toward the observatory. He thought the kids needed a break from lectures on ethics and morality, from science, experiments, internships, and athletics. They needed awe, something sublime. Maybe he needed a break too, from his teaching, from what Sonja had ordered him to do.

He opened the door to the observatory and let the students enter. Their eyes all tracked upward, from the chair at the bottom of a massive telescope forty feet to the end of the telescope, which pointed through the open ceiling and out into the night sky. He gestured for each one to sit in the chair at the front of the telescope and look through the lens.

Palmer had spent many nights that summer sitting in that chair, examining impact craters on the moon's rugged surface. Tonight, the telescope was pointed at the Sea of Tranquility, the site of the Apollo 11 landing in 1969. During his visits, Palmer looked deep into space and examined nebulae, such as the Eagle Nebula, where he could see the early formation of stars budding off from giant gas clouds. Exploring the cosmos was thrilling yet relaxing at the same time. Above all, it gave Palmer perspective on his life—his home, the Earth, which the astronomer Carl Sagan had called the *Pale Blue Dot*.

"Growing up, one of my idols was Carl Sagan," Palmer told the students as they took turns peering through the telescope. "Sagan said astronomy was humbling and character-building. For him, studying astronomy put human existence into perspective."

Palmer gazed up through the roof at the night sky. "Sagan was at NASA headquarters when the Voyager space probe was 3.7 billion miles from Earth. As the Voyager was leaving our solar system, Sagan asked the engineers to turn the satellite around and take a picture of Earth."

Monty ran his hand along the telescope's smooth metal exterior. "Must've looked pretty small from that far away."

"Earth was so tiny that it was obscured by a beam of light," Palmer replied. "Sagan talked about this photograph in a speech. He said, 'There is perhaps no better demonstration of the folly of human conceits than this distant image of our tiny world . . . it underscores our responsibility to deal more kindly with one another, and to preserve and cherish the Pale Blue Dot, the only home we've ever known.'"

CHAPTER TWENTY-ONE

Near midnight, Sonja stood at the railing of her balcony on the third floor and watched Edwin drive golf balls into the ocean. It was the perfect moment to remove him from the student population. She nodded to Mr. Aldrich, who stood three stories below. Receiving the signal, he and two guards marched toward Edwin. Though Sonja was high up, the group wasn't far away, and she faintly heard the encounter.

"Mr. Thompson, we need you to come with us right now," Mr. Aldrich said. "Dr. Woodward and Dr. Reid would like to see you in the lab."

Edwin didn't turn to face the guards. Ignoring the order, he lifted his club and swung through the ball, striking it perfectly. "It's a little late for a teacher-student conference, don't you think?"

Mr. Aldrich spoke more firmly this time. "Drop the club and follow us to Moralis, now."

Edwin faced the men and leaned against his club. "I guess it's time to pay the piper for my little stunt in class, huh?"

Mr. Aldrich stepped aside and stretched his arm out toward Moralis.

Edwin dropped the club and followed the guards. "This isn't my first run-in with authority, I get it."

Sonja watched Mr. Aldrich stay behind as his guards escorted Monty through the front doors of Moralis. Mr. Aldrich picked up Edwin's golf club and flipped it end over end in his hands. Then he turned and launched the club into the dark ocean.

Through a glass window in the exam room door, Palmer watched Mr. Aldrich and his two guards approach, with Edwin in tow. He took a deep breath and unlocked the door with his keycard.

The pressurized door swung open. "He's all yours, Dr. Reid," Mr. Aldrich said, nudging Edwin forward with one hand.

"Thank you," Palmer replied. "That will be all, gentlemen."

A guard handed Palmer Edwin's cell phone, which he slid into a pocket of his white coat. The security team left, and the door hissed shut.

There was a sink in one corner of the room, a computer on one end, and a chair with straps on the armrests and footrest near the back. Jessica stood near the chair. She, too, was wearing a white coat, and her hair was pinned up in a bun.

"I hate to break it to you," Edwin said, "but my annual physical isn't due for another six months."

Palmer pointed to the chair. “Please have a seat, Edwin.”

Edwin flopped into the metal chair, and Jessica strapped his arms and legs to the chair.

“So . . . I’m guessing you’re not going to slap my wrist with a ruler.”

Near the sink, Palmer opened a silver briefcase and retrieved from it a thin container about the size of a credit card. He inverted it a few times to swish around the reddish gel inside. He tore open another plastic container and removed a syringe.

Edwin fidgeted in the chair. “I’m not sure what this is, Dr. Reid, but isn’t there, like, a detention option, instead?”

Remaining quiet, Palmer plunged the tip of the syringe into a port on the side of the plastic container. He inverted the container and pulled back the syringe’s plunger. A clear liquid filled it. He squirted a bit into the sink, then turned to face Edwin.

Edwin’s eyes darted to the left and right. “Hey, I know I shouldn’t have messed with Wayne’s presentation, but—”

“Just try to remain still.” Jessica placed a hand on Edwin’s shoulder. “Everything’s going to be fine.”

Edwin’s eyes widened as Palmer tapped the inside of his arm to find a vein.

“I thought you were a philosophy teacher.”

“I’m also a licensed psychiatrist, Edwin.”

Edwin yanked his arms against the straps. “What kind of school is this?”

Jessica bent over Edwin and held his arm still while Palmer hovered over him with the syringe.

“This is nuts. I need to call my parents. They are not going to be cool with this—”

Sonja's voice boomed through speakers in the ceiling. "Your parents are aware of what's happening, Mr. Thompson."

Palmer knew she was watching everything through a surveillance camera, but he had wanted her to stay quiet.

Palmer faked a smile for Edwin. "Your parents authorized this, Edwin."

"We had hoped you'd respond in the classroom," Sonja continued. "Since you did not, we are advancing to the next phase of the curriculum."

"Give me more time, Dr. Woodward, please. I'll try harder, I promise." Edwin stared at the syringe. "What the hell is that, anyway?"

"The injection contains chemicals that will silence genetic errors associated with your lack of empathy," Sonja said.

"Just relax, Edwin," Jessica whispered.

Edwin's face contorted with frustration. "I'll *relax* when Dr. Frankenstein takes that goo away from my arm!"

Through the speaker, Sonja sighed heavily. "You seem to have a penchant for making things difficult."

Two guards marched into the exam room. Behind them, Mr. Aldrich watched as they pressed Edwin's writhing body back against the chair. Jessica pressed a hand against his forehead, pinning the back of his head to the headrest.

Edwin was breathing heavily. "C'mon, Teach," Edwin said, desperate. "We were just messing around in class."

Palmer couldn't meet Edwin's eyes.

"You're my teacher, Dr. Reid," Edwin pleaded. "You're supposed to guide me, protect me."

Palmer placed a hand on Edwin's shoulder. "When you wake up, you won't remember any of this."

Over the speaker, the room filled with Sonja's voice. "Initiate the treatment, Dr. Reid."

Palmer stared at the floor, feeling woozy and confused. If he didn't administer the treatment, Sonja would fire him and kick him off the island. But he knew this wasn't the right thing to do. If he plunged that syringe into Edwin's arm, he would be lost.

Damned if you do; damned if you don't.

Palmer could almost feel Sonja's impatience through the camera. "Dr. Reid, administer the treatment!"

Palmer took a deep breath, eyed the vein in Edwin's arm, and slid the needle home. He depressed the plunger fully, and Edwin's eyelids drooped. His eyes fluttered shut, and his head slumped to the side.

CHAPTER TWENTY-TWO

Richard opened his eyes to see Loretta standing over his bed. She said his name, but her voice sounded far away. "Richard?" She pressed a hand against his shoulder. "Can you hear me?"

Regaining consciousness, Richard remembered what he and Elizabeth had done the night before. He looked at the prescription pill bottle standing open on his nightstand and the white pills scattered across the surface.

He flipped over in bed and shook Elizabeth.

"Elizabeth!"

She didn't move.

"What have you done?" Loretta asked.

Elizabeth's eyes fluttered open.

"Liz?" Richard said fondly. "Oh, thank God."

Elizabeth looked confused. "What . . . what happened?"

"We woke up," Richard said, wondering how he could've gotten the dosage wrong.

"Sir, it's about Monty. I know where he is."

Richard had always admired Loretta's ability to compartmentalize.

"Tell me where my son is," Richard commanded.

"He's on Nantucket," Loretta said. "I confirmed with the ferry company that he traveled to the island at the beginning of the summer."

She handed Richard a printed copy of an email. Richard scanned what looked to be an email from Woodward Academy. "Are these results from that ethical prediction test from—"

Loretta nodded. "Sonja Woodward."

Richard kept reading. "Positive?" He shook his head. "No, that can't be true."

"You're right, actually. Those aren't Monty's test results."

Elizabeth leaned closer. "What's going on, Loretta?"

"These results are for Joseph Hayward, a classmate of Monty's. I've already questioned Mr. Hayward. Monty went to Woodward under Joseph's name."

"But why would he do that?" Richard asked. "That place is for future criminals—not Monty. And why would he leave without saying anything?"

"Maybe he thinks he belongs there," Elizabeth said.

"Why would he think that?"

Saying nothing, Elizabeth turned on the television. The news was playing another story about Richard's fraud. She looked at her husband and raised her eyebrows.

Richard turned to Loretta. "Go to Nantucket. Find out what you can."

Richard laid his head down on a pillow. Why would Monty think he belonged at Woodward? He was an honors student, an Eagle Scout, a *good* kid.

Was this my influence? My parenting style? My personality?

Richard wondered how lying for so many years, living a double life, might have affected his boy. He wondered what Monty had thought when he'd first discovered the truth. Did it come as no surprise to him? Or had it blown his world apart? And what did Monty think of him now? Did he despise him? Pity him? Want nothing to do with him?

CHAPTER TWENTY-THREE

At the Nantucket Cottage Hospital, Dr. Sax led Monty and the other interns from the emergency room to the intensive care unit. They entered an exam room, and Dr. Sax greeted the elderly man waiting inside. When asked if he was comfortable having students in the room, the man nodded. Dr. Sax asked about the man's symptoms, took down his family history, and then performed a physical exam.

Dr. Sax pressed a stethoscope against the old man's chest to listen to his heart. He then turned to the students. "The most important tool we have as physicians is to listen."

Dr. Sax handed the stethoscope to Monty. Using it, Monty heard the soft lub-dub, lub-dub, lub-dub of the man's heartbeat.

"The heart pumps over a million times in a lifetime," Dr. Sax said. "It's always pumping: no breaks, no vacations, not even a sick day."

A remarkable organ, Monty thought. *A miracle.*

Dr. Sax showed the students how to calculate heart rate. He instructed Monty to press two fingers to the man's wrist, where the ulnar artery lay beneath the skin, and to watch the clock while counting the pulses. After thirty seconds, Monty had counted 30 pulses. He then multiplied that by two to determine that the man's heart rate was 60 beats per minute.

Fifteen minutes later, Monty could still hear the lub-dub, lub-dub ringing in his ears when the group reached the exam room where Laura's grandmother was staying. Several feet from the room, Dr. Sax turned to the interns. "Since her diagnosis two months ago, Mrs. Caldwell's lung cancer has moved to her liver. I've ordered a CT scan to check for tumors in her brain."

"Treatment options?" one intern asked.

"She's on a cancer therapy called Avastia."

Monty raised his hand reflexively. "You're still prescribing Avastia?"

Surely Dr. Sax was aware of his father's fraud case. It had been all over the news. Avastia was ineffective, and might even be dangerous.

"As long as Avastia is still on the market, I will continue prescribing it to patients who have little hope otherwise."

Hope is a double-edged sword, Monty thought.

Hope can keep us buoyant, but it can also lead us down dangerous paths. Had hope driven his father to commit fraud? Hope that Avastia would show efficacy in the research even when it became clear that it would not. Hope that Avastia wouldn't be harmful in animals, in humans, even though results had proved otherwise. Hope that Richard could make up a few numbers and graphs until a new clinical trial bailed him out of the mess he'd gotten himself into. Hope that the truth of the scandal wouldn't be discovered.

As Dr. Sax and the others continued down the hallway, Monty stopped at the door to Mrs. Caldwell's room and poked his head in. The elderly woman was sleeping. Laura sat in a chair in the corner, reading quietly, a pair of headphones in her ears. She perked up when she saw him.

Monty smiled and walked into the room. "What are you listening to?"

Laura waved him closer. She pulled an earbud from one ear and handed it to Monty. He knelt beside her and inserted it in his own ear.

Monty heard the distinct sound of whales communicating with each other.

The most important tool we have as physicians is to listen.

"They're humpback whales," Laura said.

The sounds were high-pitched and ghostly, eerily beautiful. "What are they 'saying'?"

"They're singing." A smile spread across Laura's face. "A whale can hear the song of another whale from a thousand miles away."

Monty removed the earbud and handed it back to Laura. "You said your grandfather was a whaler?"

"He was from one of Nantucket's founding families. This island used to be the foremost whaling port in the world. In the first half of the twentieth century, thousands of whales were killed, reduced to oil, blubber, and meat. It brought great wealth to the island, but it nearly wiped out every species of whale."

"What happened to your grandfather?"

"After a long, successful career as a whaler, one day, he just gave it all up."

"Why?"

Laura looked at her grandmother, asleep in the bed. "My grandmother played him this recording of whales singing. After that, my grandfather knew he could never kill another whale."

Monty found Laura enchanting—the curls in her brown hair, the warm glow to her olive-colored skin. Her voice was soft and dignified. He barely knew her, but he had the urge to kiss her.

"He also helped stop the hunting by petitioning for a global ban. In 1966, a few years after he gave up whaling, the humpback whale became a protected species."

Monty remembered Dr. Sax and the others then and knew he had to get back to the rounds. He stood up quickly, excusing himself. Before leaving, he asked, "Would you like to visit Woodward tomorrow?"

"What's at Woodward?" she asked.

"A rowing competition."

Laura smiled and put the second earbud back in her ear. "I'll see you there, Monty." Then she closed her eyes as Monty left.

Not far from the ocean, a couple hundred spectators were spread out on a sand dune with beach towels and reclining chairs. Some were Nantucket residents; others had traveled from Cape Cod. Most had brought snacks and drinks and were reading newspapers or books, waiting for the Nantucket Regatta to begin.

"The locals want to see their kids pummel the Woodward students," Coach Bode said, standing beside Monty.

"We'll see about that," Monty said.

Laura was sitting in a beach chair, wearing a colorful bathing suit and a hat to shield her from the sun. She lifted her head from her book, met Monty's eyes, and waved. Monty returned the wave and continued to scan the crowd for Edwin.

They had trained for this rowing competition all summer, and Edwin was missing. Edwin hadn't been in his bed when Monty woke that morning. He hadn't been at breakfast and hadn't attended class. Monty had even asked Palmer, who'd said, "He isn't feeling well," and continued grading papers at his desk.

Now, they had five minutes to get their boat in the water, or they would be disqualified. If Edwin didn't show, all of their work would be for nothing.

"Where's Edwin?" Coach Bode asked.

"Good question."

"Well, he's got four minutes until the gun goes off."

"How cold is the water today, Coach?"

"Super cold, forty degrees." Coach Bode nudged Monty with his shoulder. "Let's avoid those crabs and stay in the boat, all right?"

Monty smirked, then locked eyes with the rowing captain who had beat him in a sprint a few weeks prior. The boy grinned and pulled back his right leg, stretching a muscular quadricep.

A voice came from behind Monty, almost formal in tone. "Hello, Monty."

Monty spun around to find Edwin dressed in his rowing uniform, holding his hands together behind his back. His voice sounded strangely passive.

"Two minutes!" yelled the referee through a megaphone from his place on the shore.

"Let's go, man!" Monty grabbed Edwin's shoulder and ran onto the dock. With one foot on the dock and the other inside their boat, Monty held the boat steady and Edwin took his place at the aft. Settled, Edwin held the dock to keep the boat still and Monty boarded the stern. Grabbing their oars, they rowed their boat in between two others from Nantucket High School.

Waiting for the gun to fire, Monty looked over his shoulder at the mile of calm ocean water that they would soon cover. Monty turned and smiled at Laura, and then took a deep breath and relaxed his shoulders.

The crack of the gun echoed across the water.

Monty and Edwin both leaned forward. In tandem, they pushed the paddles of their oars back, caught the ocean water, and heaved their bodies backward, propelling the boat away from the start line.

"Sync up, guys!" Coach Bode yelled from his motorboat about a hundred feet away.

Monty and Edwin found a rhythm pulling together, and the boat picked up speed. Monty's lungs burned. Between deep breaths, he gasped out, "C'mon, Edwin, we can catch them!"

Their boat was ten feet behind Nantucket High School's, the one containing the captain. The two pulled together, their oars catching and releasing the water at the same time. It felt as if their legs, arms, and backs were contracting simultaneously. *We're in sync,* Monty thought.

The two boats inched closer together. Five feet. One foot. The front of their boat passed the back of Nantucket High's lead boat. Then Monty was beside the captain, who glanced at them with a look of disgust.

Monty and Edwin were rowing better than they ever had. Strong. Their timing was impeccable. *We might win this thing.*

Out of the corner of his eye, Monty saw the flash of an oar swinging up and then slashing the water. Nantucket High's boat had flipped violently.

"We should help them!" Edwin screamed between breaths.

"We're in swing, man," Monty protested, rowing with more force. "Their coach will help them. We're going to win!"

Though as much as Monty wanted to win, he was growing worried. Another boat blew past the upturned hull, but there was still no sign of the captain or his teammate. Were they stuck underneath the boat?

Ignoring Monty, Edwin lowered his oar into the water and turned his paddle to grab water, creating resistance. The boat slowed and began to turn to the right.

"What are you doing?" Monty looked over his shoulder. He was surprised to see that Edwin seemed to be in genuine distress, as if he were the one struggling for air underneath the water. It even looked like he might cry.

"We've got to go help them," Edwin said.

Monty couldn't row while Edwin was using his oar to turn the boat, so he gave in and helped Edwin spin them. They rowed toward the capsized boat. Fifteen seconds later, they pulled up beside it. The captain's teammate had surfaced and was coughing up water, weakly clinging to the bottom of the boat. The captain was still nowhere in sight. By then, it must have been two minutes since he'd gone under.

Monty didn't hesitate. He slid out of his seat and into the frigid water. Under the surface, he opened his eyes and swam to the Nantucket High boat and saw two legs kicking frantically beneath it.

Monty thrust his body forward. The captain's hand was caught underneath the boat's seat. Through the murky ocean water, Monty saw the captain's wide, terrified eyes. Monty reached for his trapped hand, but just then, Edwin rammed into Monty from behind and swam past him. Monty watched Edwin grab the boy's hand and tug hard, but nothing budged. Edwin tugged again without success. And again, and nothing.

When Edwin pulled a fourth time, Monty yanked down on the boat's seat. The captain's hand slid free. The three of them swam violently toward the surface. As soon as their heads hit the air, they all gasped.

"Let's get them out of the water," Coach Bode shouted from his motorboat.

Monty coughed and treaded water. He fuzzily saw Coach Bode reach toward him. "C'mon. Get in the boat, Monty."

Monty shook his head and swam toward the Nantucket High captain, who looked shocked that Monty hadn't boarded his coach's boat.

"Why don't we get back in our boats and finish this race?" Monty asked.

The captain, still coughing up ocean water, blinked his eyes. Treading water, he seemed to consider Monty's words for a moment and then nodded.

The coaches were beside themselves. "What the hell are you guys doing?" the Nantucket High's coach yelled.

Edwin looked just as surprised. "Shouldn't we get him to the hospital?"

Monty ignored everyone and worked with the captain to flip his boat upright. Then he helped both athletes into their seats. Nearly out of breath, the captain thanked Monty, who turned and swam toward his own boat. He climbed in with Edwin's help.

"I don't know what we're doing, man." Edwin climbed into the boat while Monty stabilized it. "The race is over."

When everyone was settled with oars in hand, Monty looked over at the Nantucket High captain and nodded. Both boats began to move slowly. They picked up speed and crawled toward the finish line.

When the boats approached the finish, the crowd went berserk, applauding and cheering. Coach Bode and even the other coach joined in and clapped.

The two boats passed the finish line side by side. There was no obvious winner. Monty and Edwin cheered. The Nantucket High boat steered close to them, and the four athletes gave each other high fives.

From the shore, Loretta snapped a picture of Monty's face through a telephoto lens. Lowering the camera, she sent a text to Richard.

I found your son.

CHAPTER TWENTY-FOUR

Slumped in his wheelchair, Richard watched through the front window as Loretta stepped out of her car and waded through the reporters filling his driveway. Wincing with every push, Richard wheeled himself to the front door. Since he had last visited the hospital, the ache in his side had become a stabbing pain, a near-constant reminder of his impending death.

Loretta passed Richard and placed a manila folder on the dining room table. Richard followed her and pulled the folder toward him. "What's this?"

Loretta gestured for him to open it.

Doing so, Richard picked up a photograph of Monty rowing in what looked like a competition. "You took these on Nantucket?"

Loretta nodded.

"At Woodward?"

She nodded again.

"I need to get to Nantucket right now," Richard said.

Loretta laughed, then quickly covered her mouth. She

looked down at Richard's ankle monitor and lowered her voice so Holiday in the living room wouldn't overhear her. "You're under house arrest, Richard. You're awaiting trial. The guards. The media. Leaving is not possible."

Holding his belly with one hand, Richard stood and raised a finger into the space between them. "I will not die here in this house while my son is playing water sports on Nantucket."

Loretta lowered her head and rubbed her chin. "There might be a way to get him home early. I got ahold of his file, and apparently, he's on probation. There was an incident at Nantucket Cottage Hospital. Another strike, and they'll kick him out. I could ensure he gets that strike."

Richard raised a hand. "Don't embarrass him but do whatever you have to do to get him home."

Loretta turned on her heel and walked toward the front door.

Richard lowered himself back into his wheelchair and flipped through photos that showed Monty and another student rowing together. One photo showed Monty's boat turning around; another showed Monty leaping from his boat and swimming toward an overturned boat.

Loretta's hand was on the doorknob when Richard asked, "What happened here?"

"Monty and his roommate possibly saved those two boys' lives." Loretta opened the door. "He's a remarkable young man."

Richard smiled. "Yes, he is."

CHAPTER TWENTY-FIVE

At the stern of Palmer's sailboat, Monty basked in the warm sunlight. The ocean was calm, and the sky was cloudless. Taylor and Kirsten pointed at dolphins and giggled as they swam playfully beside the boat. At the aft, Cory was sunbathing, Jonathan was glued to his phone as he made trades, and Edwin was reading quietly.

Palmer stood at the helm and navigated the boat along the Nantucket coastline. An hour before, he had steered the boat into a cove and dropped anchor to engage the class in a discussion about Seneca's book *On the Shortness of Life.*

Palmer had delivered his lecture from the boat's stern. "Many of us talk about how short life is, but Seneca thought life was actually long enough for us to do the things we want to do. What did he say the real problem was?"

"That we waste most of it," Taylor had said.

"That's right," Palmer replied. "He wrote that many of us are living, but not *really* living. Why did Seneca believe that many of us wasted our lives?"

"Because many of us experience life three times," Monty added. "Before an experience, we anticipate and worry. Next, we live the actual event. But then after the event, some tend to ruminate on the experience."

Hearing his name being called, Monty shook away the memory. He turned to see Palmer waving for Monty to join him at the helm.

When Monty got there, Palmer stepped aside. "Take the wheel, young man."

Monty wrapped his hands around the wooden wheel. For a few minutes, he held the boat on course without talking. "I've been reading and journaling," he finally said, turning to Palmer.

"Learn anything?" Palmer asked.

Monty nodded. "I'm still lost about one thing, though."

"What's that?"

"I get that life is short, right? So I should cherish time and spend it wisely on things I think are valuable. But I don't know what's valuable yet. I don't know what to spend my time on."

Palmer looked up and indicated a seagull hovering above the boat. It was floating on the wind.

"See that seagull? That bird was built to fly. Its body. Its wings. The shape of its head and beak. How it folds its legs up against its body as it glides."

"I'm not sure I understand."

"I'm saying that the bird's form—how it's built, what it's made of—dictates how it functions. A seagull has legs, sure, but it wouldn't make a good land animal. It wasn't built to run; it was built to fly."

"How does that apply to me?" Monty scanned the

other students. "To us?"

"We all have unique functions. Each of us is equipped with particular skills, abilities, and talents. Some of us are more reflective. Some are persuasive and can change minds with their ideas. We all have unique passions and desires. Jonathan is mathematical, Kirsten is artistic, Cory is athletic, Edwin is good with words. We each seem to be born with a certain temperament, an 'essence,' if you will."

"What are my talents? What's my essence?"

"I think you're the moral center of this class, but you are also a teenager of many contradictions," Palmer said, looking out to sea. "Privileged but down to earth. Innocent yet rebellious. Tenderhearted but capable of wielding a sharp tongue. There's a largeness to your character that I think will serve you well in whatever you end up doing."

"I still don't know what I want to do with my life."

"You'll figure that out as you go. Keep searching. Keep reading. Keep writing. The important part is to keep asking questions. The poet Rainer Maria Rilke once advised a young man that he should be patient with all that was left unsolved in his heart and try to love the questions. Don't seek answers; live the questions. And 'perhaps you will then gradually, without noticing it, live along some distant day into the answer.'"

Monty watched the seagull bank right, flap its wings against a headwind, and glide across the water with ease.

A few minutes later, Monty watched Edwin place his book down and stretch in his chair. Something was different about Edwin, but Monty couldn't pinpoint what. Edwin stood, walked to the side of the boat, and looked down into the water. Monty watched him lean over the railing, appearing to see something. Surprisingly, he began to cry.

Monty walked over and stood beside him. "What's wrong, Edwin?"

Edwin used his sleeve to wipe his face, then he pointed to a dead fish, bobbing on the water's surface.

"You're crying over a dead fish?" Monty asked.

"Do you ever wonder if animals can feel pain?"

Monty narrowed his eyes. "Are you feeling all right, man?"

"What do you mean?"

"You've been acting kind of weird. More emotional, I guess."

"I haven't needed to take my anti-anxiety medication, so I guess that's an improvement. But, I don't know, it's like I feel things way more deeply than I used to. I feel everything." Edwin pointed to the book near his chair. "I was crying all night reading that book in my bed last night."

Had the school's teachings worked? Monty thought.

"My parents would be happy to see me feel so much," Edwin said. "They refer to me as their little liar to their friends."

"Why?"

"I fudged some facts in a newspaper article I wrote for the *Cambridge Chronicle*. I didn't think the story was interesting enough, so I made up some quotes, invented a twist in the story. If the story hadn't gone nationwide, no one would have noticed."

Just then, Monty remembered a moment from

childhood. "When I was a kid, I was outside playing the game 'king of the hill' on the playground. My parents were watching from the edge of the playground. There was this bigger kid, older than all of us, at the top of the hill. No one could knock him off. He knocked me down a few times. I fell to the ground hard once, cutting my elbow. My mom ran and consoled me, but my dad ran over to the bully."

"What did he say to him?"

"He congratulated the bully, told him that he would be very successful someday."

"How'd that make you feel?"

"Even then, he felt like someone else's dad. The bully's dad, not mine."

In that moment, Monty felt compelled to tell Edwin everything. Sonja and Palmer already knew about his father. What's the difference if his roommate knows? And so, Monty took a deep breath and told Edwin about his real identity, his father's crime, and why he had chosen to come to Nantucket.

As Monty spoke, Edwin's eyes welled up with tears and he began crying.

CHAPTER TWENTY-SIX

After an early-morning rowing practice on Saturday, Monty showered and rode the shuttle to the hospital—not for his internship, but to visit Laura. However, she wasn't in her grandmother's room when Monty entered. Instead, a nurse was tending to an IV bag hanging above the sleeping elderly woman.

Monty bit his lip, wondering if he should . . .

"Is that Avastia?" he asked the nurse.

"It's just intravenous solution, not much more than saltwater," the nurse said, without turning. "Avastia wasn't working."

She must be declining, Monty thought. "How is she doing?"

"I probably shouldn't be telling you this, but her blood work has improved since stopping Avastia." The nurse smiled at the resting woman. "Her immune system is fighting the cancer, maybe even winning."

The nurse finished with the bag and left the room. Monty stayed, noticing that Mrs. Caldwell's face was pinker, less puffy. He watched her breathe deeply and slowly, peacefully.

Monty thought about what a life in medicine would be like. The decade-long training, the hundred-hour work-weeks, the stark reminders of life's fragility. Growing up with his father, he had seen the profound personal sacrifices involved: the despair after lost battles against an illness, phone calls at two in the morning, missed family vacations, ferocious back pain after a 12-hour shift.

It might be tempting to choose an easier path, Monty thought, but amid the stress, pain, and tragedy, there were also triumphs: A patient's seizures stop. A CT scan is clear. He remembered resuscitating Mrs. Caldwell and feeling a wave of relief upon hearing the soft, subtle beep of her revived heartbeat. To protect life was a calling. A life in medicine wasn't just a commitment to technical excellence but also moral excellence. We don't choose medicine. It chooses us.

Monty felt as if medicine was calling him.

Just then, Mrs. Caldwell's eyes flickered open. Her gaze landed on him. "Monty?"

She knows my name? So far, she'd been unconscious every time he had visited her in the hospital with Dr. Sax. Maybe she recognized him from the ambulance.

She must have noticed Monty's surprise. "I may have been unconscious, but I could hear you all. Not all the time and not every conversation, but I remember my doctor, Dr. Sax, and I remember you, Monty."

Monty had heard his father talk about patients in comas who had sustained a semiconscious state and could hear the words of their loved ones when they visited. He wondered if she had heard him interacting with Laura.

"You brought me back to life," she said.

With a twinge of shame, Monty lowered his head. "I know you had a DNR. It wasn't right of me to make that decision for you."

Mrs. Caldwell turned her head to look at a framed picture of her deceased husband that stood on the table beside her. She stayed silent, but Monty sensed that she was actually thankful to be alive. She turned to Monty and smiled.

"She's not here, Monty. You might want to try St. Mary's Church in city center."

Monty blushed, not knowing what to say.

He turned to leave, but Mrs. Caldwell stopped him. "Monty?" When he turned to her, she waved him over. "Come here, young man."

Monty approached the bed. She motioned for him to lean over. When Monty lowered his head, she placed her hands on either side of his face and kissed him softly on the forehead. Then she leaned back on the bed. "Thank you."

Monty rode the shuttle to Nantucket city center and stopped at the church. When he entered, he saw Laura kneeling in front of a statue of Christ. He knelt beside her. "I think your prayers are working."

Laura turned and smiled. "How can you know that?"

"The nurse says your grandmother is recovering."

Laura wrapped her arms around Monty. Holding him tightly, she said, "I still don't understand why you're at Woodward. You're not like the kids they talk about in the news."

Laura leaned back and let him go. Looking at him with soft, kind eyes, she continued. "I see so much good in you, but something is always bugging you. There's pain in your eyes. A hum that's always in the background."

Monty studied the floor. "I'm searching for something, I guess." He reached into his pocket and pulled out a gift he'd bought for Laura: A sculpture of a whale.

Laura smiled. "Let's go have a Saturday adventure."

Monty and Laura strolled down Upper Main Street and into Nantucket's city center, holding hands as they passed cafés, old-fashioned inns, galleries, and souvenir shops. They dipped in and out of stores, trying chocolates and salt water taffy. They walked into Mitchell's Book Corner on Main Street and pulled books from the shelves to read passages aloud to each other. Monty read a few passages from *When Breath Becomes Air*, a memoir by Paul Kalanithi, who was battling stage IV lung cancer while he wrote the book.

An hour later, they rented bikes and rode past salty ponds and along the ocean, passing picnickers, cranberry bogs, Cape Cod–styled cottages, and lighthouses. They stopped at a scenic vista and watched a sailboat tip sideways beneath a strong wind. Walking along the docks, they watched fishermen scale, gut, and season fish for hungry tourists, who took their catch to their tables. They had lunch at a restaurant ten feet from the ocean and ate fresh-caught bluefish and seaweed pudding. Afterward, they spread out on a patch of sand on the beach, gazed up at the clouds, and took turns deciding what animals the clouds looked like.

Returning to the city center, they visited the Nantucket Whaling Museum. Inside, they admired the massive skeleton of a whale that hung from the ceiling. Laura stopped at one exhibit and read the plaque. "This says that blue whales sleep by taking very short naps while slowly swimming close to the ocean's surface." She explained that this was called *logging*. "They sleep at the surface because they have to remember to open their blowholes to breathe." Her eyes bright with curiosity, Laura continued: "Blue whales can never completely lose consciousness, not even in sleep; otherwise, they would drown."

In another room, there was a model of a humpback whale caught in a fishing net. A voice narrated the scene through a speaker: "The noise of human-made vessels can disorient and sometimes traumatize these magnificent creatures, even precipitate a kind of psychosis."

Laura bumped Monty with her hip. "Is that what Woodward's like?"

Monty chuckled as he considered the idea that he had spent the summer caught in a fishing net, though he knew he had been caught in a net well before he ever arrived there. Yet slowly, painstakingly, his time at this unusual school for the "predisposed" had helped him cut away knots and release gnarled rope. With every moral lesson or cautionary tale in class, every examination of his problems with Palmer, and every self-reflection he processed in his journal or while reading, Monty felt freer from the net, able to swim unsnarled, able to be himself and become who he really was.

Monty and Laura dipped into another room. Monty wrapped his arm around Laura's lower back as they sidestepped another visitor. Laura told Monty that she was going to Emerson College in the fall to study poetry. Monty shared that he had gotten into Harvard and would probably study premed and go to Harvard Medical School, like his father. After medical school, maybe he would join Doctors Without Borders.

Monty told Laura that he was captivated by a book he had stumbled upon one night in his father's library. It was called *Mountains Beyond Mountains* and followed the physician Paul Farmer and his heroic efforts to solve public health crises in impoverished countries. "Chemistry classes and lab experiments don't inspire me to become a doctor," Monty said, "but Paul Farmer does. He cares about the patient."

"For someone who's not supposed to feel the emotions of others, you sure do have a lot of empathy."

"I know what medicine means; I just don't know exactly why I should follow that path."

"You have time. You don't have to figure out your whole life this afternoon."

Laura's words comforted Monty. Few people seemed to support the challenging quest to find one's place in the world. An authentic fit. Monty's classmates urged him to pick a college major and find a career path quickly. Yet some of them were just as lost as he was. They impulsively chose careers in law or medicine as an antidote to an uncertain future. Even though they had no connection to such careers, no talent for their chosen field of interest, some committed themselves to cutting their teeth on Wall Street, getting into management consulting at McKinsey, earning an MBA, or snagging a job that paid over $100K, all to be millionaires by the age of thirty.

At sunset, Monty and Laura ate ice cream and watched

a summertime concert on the shore. Later, while walking, Monty told Laura about Palmer's teachings: How he was opening Monty's mind and getting him and the other students to think about themselves and the world in new and exciting ways. There was a whole moral dimension to life that many of them had never considered.

"You know, Aristotle thought that contemplation was the highest form of moral activity," Monty mused as they strolled through a small park.

Laura stopped in front of the granite bust of a famous writer. She placed her hands on his shoulders. "Montgomery, the philosopher. I like it."

Later in the evening, they sat on the beach and let the waves lap at their toes. Laura slid her hand under Monty's arm and clutched him gently, laying her head on his shoulder.

Monty loved the gentle pressure of Laura leaning against him. He couldn't stop smiling. His chest feeling full, he took a deep breath. "Do you want to come to the Woodward dance with me next week?"

Laura snapped her head up to stare at Monty through hooded eyes. "I would love that."

Monty leaned forward and kissed Laura softly. For a few minutes, they continued kissing, moving their hands around each other's bodies. When they finally broke apart, they saw a group of people nearby using matches to light paper lanterns. Once lit, the lanterns floated upward, illuminating a dark patch of the night sky.

Laura popped up from the sand and, clutching Monty's hand, jogged toward the group of people on the beach.

"Can we try?" Laura asked the man who was giving out lanterns to the others.

"Of course," the man said and handed Laura and Monty matches and two lanterns. "Before you light the candle," he told them, "think of a worry or anxiety. As you watch your lantern float away, imagine that worry floating away with it." He pointed to a middle-aged man who was watching his lantern as it floated perhaps 40 feet above the beach. "He's forgiving his wife. He's unburdening himself. Otherwise, it would make him sick."

Monty and Laura took their lanterns to the water's edge.

Laura handed Monty a match. "Are you thinking of something?"

Monty nodded. At that moment, he could only think of one thing, one person. His father. His fraud, his deception. Monty wasn't ready to forgive his father. Not yet, not tonight. But maybe someday. Maybe before the cancer took his life.

Monty and Laura knelt and used the matches to light the candles inside the lanterns. Slowly, the lanterns floated off the sand and caught the breeze. Monty wrapped an arm around Laura, and they watched the lanterns glow above the ocean.

Monty and Laura took an Uber to the Hughes' vacation home on the east side of the island. In the car, Monty described how his father had bought the beach cottage when he was eight years old. "My family visits it every summer." After a momentary hesitation, he added, "Except this summer."

When they arrived, Monty flipped over a clamshell beside the front door to reveal a key. Unlocking the door, he took Laura's hand and led her into the 500-square-foot cottage.

"Watch your head," he said, sidestepping a spiral staircase in the center of the living room. The staircase wound up to a loft that held a bed, a nightstand, and a rocking chair. Monty had spent many hours up there, reading and writing.

Laura took in the cottage's open floor plan as she walked from the small living room into the kitchen. "This place is so cozy." She wandered over to a bookcase and admired a trophy that stood on the top shelf. The sculpture resembled a downhill skier, and the base bore the engraving "Most Improved."

Monty walked over and nodded to the trophy. "In seventh grade, I crashed hard on my first run and got last place."

"Why'd you crash?"

"I like to go fast." He grinned. "Turns out, if I didn't crash, I won."

"How often did you crash after that first run?"

"I didn't."

Laura chuckled. "Most improved." She kissed Monty tenderly. "I'm really glad you came into my life."

Monty wrapped his arms around her and squeezed her close.

Laura bit her lip before speaking again. "I have to show you something," she said, her voice shaky.

"What is it?" Monty led her to the couch, and they sat down, holding hands.

Laura pulled her phone from her pocket. "Remember

when I played you a recording of whales singing in the hospital?"

Monty nodded.

"After, I found a strand of your hair on my shirt." She looked at the ground. "I sort of . . . well, tested it."

"Tested it?"

"I asked my uncle at Moralis Labs to test your DNA."

Monty gasped. "Why would you do that?"

"Because I knew you didn't belong at Woodward. And look!" Laura turned her phone to show Monty his results. "It says you tested negative. You *have* the empathy genes."

Monty stood, his face flushed, and leaned a hand against the stairwell. He knew he scored negative. Should he tell her who he really was? The real reason he was on Nantucket, at Woodward? With her? That he had lied his way into the academy?

Monty grabbed a framed photograph of him and his father standing together in the hallway of a hospital. "Do you recognize the man in this picture?"

Laura shook her head.

"His name is Richard Hughes. This man is my father."

"But your last name is—?"

"My last name is Hughes, not Hayward. My name is Montgomery Hughes." He sighed. "I used a friend's positive test results to get into Woodward."

"I don't understand. Why would you want to come here?"

Monty pointed to his father in the photo. "Because I came from *him*. I'm not one of the 'good ones,' Laura." He shook his head. "You know that drug your grandmother was on?"

Laura narrowed her eyes.

"My father's biotech company made Avastia. An employee told me that the drug was a fake—that it was unsafe—before it went to market. Yet I did nothing."

"You knew it was dangerous while my grandmother was on it?"

Monty averted his eyes to avoid the pained expression on Laura's face.

"Why didn't you say something to Dr. Sax?"

"Because I'm a coward, all right!" Monty looked at the picture again. "Because I've got that man's blood in my veins." He pointed at Laura's phone. "I don't need some lab results to tell me I should be at Woodward. I *know* I should be here."

Laura stood up from the couch. "What else are you hiding?"

"I've told you everything."

Laura opened the Uber app on her phone. "I'm leaving," she said as she ordered a ride.

"Laura, c'mon. Don't go," Monty pleaded.

Laura waved her hand and walked out to the driveway. When her car arrived, she hopped in, and it sped off.

Monty sank down onto the couch and scrubbed his face with his hands. Just as he was losing himself in despair, he remembered something Laura had said: "Keep your eyes open" at Woodward. She had mentioned her uncle's suspicions about Moralis. Monty pulled his phone from his pocket. He googled Sonja Woodward and read articles from *WIRED* magazine, *The New York Times*, and *Forbes*, praising Sonja for her business acumen and vision as a scientist. He scrolled through search results. The title of one article, posted a week before, by Amy Baker piqued his interest: "Intellectual Property Debate Over Infamous Cancer Drug."

Monty was a paragraph into the article when his mouth dropped open.

The article was about Sonja's experience as a doctoral student at Harvard. There had been a controversy between her and Richard Hughes, where he was an MD/PhD student. As Monty's eyes skimmed down the page, he learned that Sonja and his father had worked together on a "novel epigenetic inhibitor for difficult-to-treat cancers."

Avastia.

"Court records show that Sonja Woodward claimed that she invented the bromodomain inhibitor with little collaboration or input from Richard Hughes, and yet records show that Dr. Hughes filed the patent under his name only."

Reading on, Monty learned that his father had been accused of stealing ownership of the intellectual property behind Avastia, the drug on which he had built Nautilus. His career. His life. Near the end, the article stated, "Several years after the alleged intellectual theft, Dr. Woodward left the field of cancer biology to lead the burgeoning field of behavioral genetics with the explicit goal to understand the genetic and molecular underpinnings of amoral behavior."

Sonja had created Moralis Labs and her genetic test *because* of his father. Richard had stolen from her, cheated her, but it seemed he had also inspired within her a dark passion, a crusade to stop immoral people like Richard Hughes.

Monty closed the browser and realized he had several unread messages in a group chat with his classmates. Kirsten had sent a picture of a massive pirate ship that she had apparently spray-painted on the wall of Woodward's main administration building.

"Oh my God," Taylor had written. "Did you do that?"

Kirsten had inserted an emoji of a woman shrugging.

Below the text was a line Monty recognized from Moby Dick: "For there is no folly of the beast of the earth which is not infinitely outdone by the madness of men."

Monty scrolled through more responses only to see that Kirsten had stopped responding in the last several hours. The text messages turned from amusement to worry.

"Missed you at dinner, Kirsten," Jonathan wrote with an emoji of a man crying.

A couple hours later, Cory wrote, "Um, hello? Earth to Kirsten? Where are you?"

"Okay, guys, I'm kind of worried," Taylor wrote. "Kirsten hasn't come back to our room yet."

Monty realized that something was wrong. Without thinking, he opened Uber and ordered a ride to campus.

CHAPTER TWENTY-SEVEN

At Moralis, Palmer ran water over his hands and splashed some across his face. As he dried his hands on a towel, he noticed they were shaking. Leaving the bathroom, he opened the high-pressure door that led into the lab and entered the exam room. He had told Jessica to take the night off, but Kirsten was there, sitting upright in the same chair Edwin had when he received his treatment.

Palmer had tried to avoid this step, had tried to warn Kirsten that if she didn't smarten up, there were consequences. But she had continued to skip classes and failed to submit essays on time. The final straw had been when she spray-painted a pirate ship on the main administrative building. An impressive piece of art, but Sonja hadn't been amused.

Palmer had stood with Sonja out on the school's main lawn as she stared up at the graffiti. "Well, Dr. Reid," she'd finally said, "I guess we have another nonresponder."

"Let's observe Edwin a bit longer," Palmer had pleaded. "See how he responds before we treat another student."

"I have a congressman visiting today. We'll do the procedure then. That way, he can see how we're spending his money."

Kirsten was in and out of consciousness, groggy with anesthesia. The drug in her system was the same that Edwin had received, and it would have an amnesiac effect. She would forget the procedure, just as Edwin had.

Standing at a desk in the exam room, Palmer prepared a vial. Any minute, Sonja would enter the viewing theater above him and order him to administer the treatment.

Just then, Palmer heard someone whisper his name. He spun around to see Monty leaning against the heavy door.

Palmer glanced nervously up at the viewing theater then back to Monty. "You shouldn't be here!"

Kirsten's eyes opened slowly. "Dr. Reid? Monty?" She scanned the room anxiously. "What's going on?"

Monty put a finger to his lips to keep Kirsten quiet, but his eyes never left his teacher. "What's in that syringe, Dr. Reid?"

"Just leave it alone, Monty."

Monty couldn't have known what was in Palmer's syringe, but he could probably tell that it went against everything that Palmer stood for.

Palmer pointed at the door. "Go!"

Ignoring him, Monty walked to a tray and filled a syringe with clear liquid. He squirted a little of the liquid onto the floor to remove any air bubbles, then placed the syringe next to the one Palmer had prepared.

"Use this syringe," Monty insisted. "It's saline."

Palmer became even more anxious. Out of the corner of his eye, he saw the door of the viewing theater open.

Sonja held it open for a man in a suit—the congressman. Palmer pushed Monty back toward the door he'd come through. Palmer watched as Monty jogged down the hallway and disappeared around a corner.

Just as Monty disappeared from Palmer's view, Sonja's voice boomed through the speaker. "Are you ready to begin, Dr. Reid?"

Palmer swallowed. "All set here, Dr. Woodward."

Sonja and the congressman stepped closer to the window. "Please proceed."

Palmer wheeled the tray over to Kirsten and stared down at the two syringes filled with clear liquid. Monty had given him an option.

A dilemma.

"Everything all right down there, Dr. Reid?"

Palmer faked a smile. "Just preparing the materials, Dr. Woodward."

Palmer's eyes darted back and forth between the syringe with saline and the syringe with the CRISPR solution.

Taking a deep breath, Palmer made a decision. Not giving himself a chance to question it, he grabbed Monty's syringe, approached Kirsten, and injected its contents into her arm.

Palmer crashed through the front doors of Moralis and crossed the courtyard. He ripped off his white coat and sat on the stone seat beside the fountain. He tilted his head back so he could look at the sky.

"Which syringe did you choose?"

Palmer turned to see Monty walk into view. "You could've gotten us both kicked out of here with that stunt," he hissed.

Monty folded his arms and held his gaze steadily.

Palmer looked away in shame, even though he felt he eventually did the right thing. "I chose yours."

Monty's shoulders relaxed, and he shook his head. "What's really going on here?"

"We're testing a treatment for students who don't respond to what we're trying to do at Woodward."

"Did you treat Edwin?"

"I did what I was told to do," Palmer said, turning away.

"That sounds awfully familiar, doesn't it, Dr. Reid." Monty narrowed his eyes. "The Nazi administrators who were 'just following orders'? The banality of evil, hmm?"

Palmer threw his hands up. "I've voiced my concerns. I've told Dr. Woodward that people are more than their genes, that gene-hacking won't fix issues caused by the environment or by one's childhood. She won't listen, though. There's too much at stake."

"Where is this pressure coming from?"

"There's a lot of money involved, Monty. Sonja will do anything to make sure Woodward doesn't fail."

Monty nodded slowly. "She's failed before. I know about her past. She and my . . ." He hesitated.

"Your father destroyed Sonja's career to launch his own." Palmer shook his head knowingly. "I saw the article in the paper. He stole Sonja's cancer cure."

"A cure that turned out to be a fake," Monty said.

Palmer nodded.

"And that's why Sonja created Moralis and her ethical prediction test. Woodward. To stop people like my father."

"You worked at his company, so you think you're complicit?"

"Aren't I?" He pointed a finger at Palmer. "Aren't you complicit too?"

"Of course I am," Palmer said. "My situation's worse, though. You didn't know what your father was doing. I know what Sonja's up to, but I don't have the guts to take my hand off the switch."

"You did the right thing today," Monty said.

"No, *you* did the right thing, Monty. But what happens when Sonja tells me to treat Cory or Taylor or Jonathan?

"Or me..."

"If that happens, I don't know what I will do."

"You will stand up to her. *We* will stand up to her."

CHAPTER TWENTY-EIGHT

"How can I help you, Mr. Thompson?" Sonja invited Edwin to sit in the chair across from her desk. As she asked that, Sonja realized that something was different about Edwin. Ever since his treatment, there was a childlike naïveté in his expression. He seemed innocent, almost too pure for this world.

"Thank you for meeting with me, Dr. Woodward." Edwin pulled a copy of *The Inquirer and Mirror* from his backpack. He handed the newspaper to Sonja and pointed at the first article on the front page. The byline included his name and Amy Baker's. "Did you read my first article yet?"

"As the head of a school and a biotech company, I'm afraid I don't have much time to keep up with the news." Sonja read the headline aloud: "Will cancer fraudster, Richard Hughes, live to see his trial?" She glanced at Edwin.

"Monty told me that *this man* was his father."

Sonja knew, of course, but she played along, wondering

where Edwin was going with this. "You're saying this man right here, Richard Hughes"—Sonja looked away for a moment, pondering—"is Monty's father?"

Edwin nodded. "Monty took the identity of a friend who scored positive."

Sonja narrowed her eyes. "Why are you bringing this to my attention, Mr. Thompson?"

Edwin rubbed his temples. "Ever since Monty told me his secret, I've had this terrible migraine. But when I decided to tell you, it faded. And now that I've told you, it's gone."

What a fascinating response to the treatment, Sonja thought.

"Monty doesn't believe in Woodward—not like I do. I think he might try to embarrass you, maybe even try to stop you."

Sonja placed a hand on Edwin's shoulder. "Thank you for your honesty."

"It felt like the right thing to do."

Sonja led him back to the door and opened it for him. He hesitated, looking like he was searching for words.

"What is it, Edwin?" Sonja said matter-of-factly.

"A few nights ago, I had a dream that felt so real. I was with you and Dr. Reid in Moralis. I dreamed there was some kind of medical procedure, but I can't remember the details."

"You're all under a lot of pressure here, so it's not surprising that your sleep is being affected. But I just want you to know that what you did here, just now, was the right thing to do. Both Dr. Reid and I have been impressed with your progress."

Edwin turned to leave but then hesitated again. "This

morning, there was a dying seal stranded on the beach. I knew if I couldn't get it into the water, it would die." His eyes filled with tears. "I tried to push it back into the ocean for over an hour. I was crying. I pushed so hard, but I couldn't save it."

The CRISPR treatment has worked brilliantly, Sonja thought.

Edwin had indeed developed empathy. In fact, it seemed that Edwin felt *everything*. Had he developed an empathy disorder? A result of an overgrowth of mirror neurons, Sonja wondered. And *how incredible* was it that Edwin had developed a physical symptom—a migraine—when he was testing the boundaries of his ethics, and yet he seemed to feel better after confessing.

Following Edwin out into the hallway, Sonja nodded at Mr. Aldrich, who stood vigil. "Monty cheated his way into my school, Edwin. He's a liar. What you did tonight represents the principles Woodward was founded on, and you should be proud."

Minutes later, Edwin was gone, and Sonja was taking a seat at her desk, opening her phone and typing the name Richard Hughes into the contacts list. She tapped Richard's name and listened as it rang.

Sonja had been waiting for this moment for years.

"Hello," said a man's voice. It sounded weak, almost muted—the opposite of that smug, overconfident voice that had burned its way into her mind in graduate school.

"May I speak with Dr. Richard Hughes, please?"

Richard coughed loudly. "Who is this?"

"You don't recognize the voice of an old friend?"

A few seconds passed. "Sonja?"

She lifted the newspaper Edwin had given her from

her desk. "I hear you've gotten yourself into trouble."

"What in God's name do you want, Sonja?"

"It's not what I want. It's what I can give you."

"I know Monty is there. Please, send him home."

"Oh, no, no, Richard. Montgomery's education isn't complete."

"He doesn't belong there. He's a good kid, nothing like me."

"You sure about that? Your son faked my genetic test; he stole the last name of a friend to get in here. Oh, no, it seems the apple doesn't fall far from the tree."

"Sonja, I know we've had our differences in the past, but that's no reason to—"

"Differences?" Sonja interrupted. "You stole my invention—the drug that Nautilus was founded on! Why do you think I studied behavioral ethics? Why do you think I created a genetic prediction test? To stop scum like you."

A few seconds passed. Then Richard said, "Sonja, I'm dying."

Like I care, Sonja thought.

"Tomorrow night, Woodward is having a dance," Sonja said. "Parents are invited, to see how far their children have come. I'm cordially inviting you to attend."

"There are a half-dozen FBI agents in my home right now."

"You discovered the cure for cancer, Dr. Hughes," Sonja said sarcastically. "You'll figure something out. Meanwhile, in light of Monty's violation of Woodward's honor code, I will have to arrange a punishment. We have ways, you know, to treat students who don't respond to our teachings."

Sonja hung up the phone. The irony was overwhelming. The son of the man who had stolen her invention had cheated his way into her school that taught ethical principles to those genetically predisposed to be amoral.

She examined the front page of the newspaper. Richard's theft had ruined her career—nearly ruined her life. Richard needed a punishment that would fit his crime. She was going to destroy the one thing he had left in his pathetic life.

Montgomery.

CHAPTER TWENTY-NINE

Agent Holiday was making his daily rounds at the Hughes residence in the morning when he noticed the empty wheelchair in the living room.

The *empty* living room.

Holiday began searching the house, his pace increasing with every empty room. Not in the kitchen, not in the dining room, not in the study. In the spare bedroom, Elizabeth was sleeping alone on the queen-size bed.

As he searched for Richard, Holiday passed other confused agents. He smashed his shoulder through the basement door, gun drawn. No sign of Richard there, either. Holiday holstered his pistol and touched his earpiece.

"I've lost contact with Dr. Hughes."

Holiday ran to the dining room, opened his laptop, and activated the GPS for Richard's ankle monitor.

"Where are you?" Holiday whispered to himself.

A blinking red dot appeared in the middle of a map on the screen. Holiday grimaced. The dot was blinking in Cape Cod near Woods Hole.

Monty left his dorm room and made his way toward Woodward's main conference hall. As he walked, a car pulled up alongside him, and the passenger-side door opened. A long green dress spilled out onto the pavement, and Laura stepped out after. Her hair was pulled up and her sleeveless dress showed off her slender arms.

After what had happened the night before in the cottage, Monty was surprised she had shown up, but he was happy to see her. And she looked stunning; he was almost breathless in her presence.

"I'm looking for a school dance," she said, grinning. "Do you know where I can find the main conference hall?"

"I'm on my way there now," Monty said. "You're welcome to join me."

Monty helped Laura step up onto the sidewalk. In heels, she grabbed his shoulder to stabilize herself. "Monty, I overreacted last night. I understand why you came here, and why you decided to hide your identity."

Monty turned and locked eyes with her.

"I know you admitted yourself to Woodward because you thought you needed help. But I want you to know that you don't need as much help as you think. You're really hard on yourself. You're all right, you know."

Not knowing how to respond, Monty looked away.

Laura bumped her hip into Monty's. "You're actually pretty great."

Thick dark clouds gathered over Nantucket as the motorboat approached the island. Loretta's hair whipped in all directions as she steered the boat. Richard gazed at the island in agony. The pain in his side was constant now. Sometimes, it was just a dull ache; other times, it was a searing pain, as though his guts were being ripped from his abdomen.

"About twenty minutes," Loretta yelled over the engine's roar. "We should make it before the storm."

Holding hands, Monty and Laura walked into Woodward's main conference hall. Students milled about, chatting. A few couples twirled on the dance floor. Around the dance floor, tables filled the rest of the hall. Parents sat at most of them, having come to see how their kids had changed, if at all. Had they successfully navigated Sonja's social experiment? Were they "rehabilitated"? Had they achieved "moral enlightenment," as the papers liked to quip?

Monty crossed the dance floor, nodding to Cory, who was pretending to do the Salsa with Taylor. "Nice moves," Monty said as he passed the two students. He spotted his name at one of the tables and pulled out a chair for Laura. There were eight people sitting at the table, including Edwin and his parents.

CHAPTER THIRTY

Sonja was admiring a plaque on the wall of her office when she heard Richard's cane clack against the hardwood floor in the hallway. The plaque listed donors who had contributed money to Woodward. Next to the plaque hung a framed quote: "The arc of the moral universe is long, but it bends toward justice." Sonja had waited so long for this encounter. Finally, she could tell Richard everything she had wanted to say—*needed* to say—since he had stolen her invention.

Entering her office, Richard's face was ashen, his back contorted over his wooden cane. He was a shadow of the man Sonja had met in graduate school. Then, two decades ago, he had been larger than life and could command the attention of everyone in a room. Now, Richard groaned as he put his weight awkwardly on his cane. Sonja did not offer him a seat. She smiled, seeing Richard in pain, nearly dead.

"A few years ago, I received a generous—*anonymous*—donation to Woodward," Sonja said. "It wasn't hard to trace that million dollars back to you."

"I came here to get Monty, not to rehash the past—"

"It's not like you to provide help and expect no credit," Sonja said, cutting him off. "I know why you did it. Our esteemed Professor, Palmer Reid, calls it 'moral compensation.' You felt guilty for stealing my invention, and you thought donating to the person you screwed over would make you feel better."

Sonja turned around to face Richard. "Well, Dr. Hughes, your deed did *not* balance the moral scorecard."

Richard's face contorted with disgust. "It's a twist of irony that you've been using my donation—the taxpayer's money—to fund your morally dubious science experiments."

How did Richard know about her CRISPR technology, Sonja thought? Apparently, Loretta was as good as Mr. Aldrich had said she was.

Richard continued. "You're a fool if you think Woodward Academy—moral education, in general—can solve society's problems."

"Only a criminal like you would want to live in a world where corporate scandals and financial crises happen repeatedly. Where athletics is spoiled by cheaters. Where parents buy their kids into colleges." Sonja slammed her fist against the wall. "I change their genes, I change the world."

"Look in the mirror, Sonja," Richard said. "We're not so different, you and me. You started Woodward to 'do good'—to use your words—because you needed a license to 'do bad' with your twisted moral enhancement campaign."

Sonja laughed. "I'm getting morality lessons from the man who committed the largest fraud in the history of medical science. You set back cancer research fifteen years. How many thousands of patients were hurt by Avastia's side effects?"

Sonja approached Richard, who seemed barely able to stay upright. She circled him like a lion about to down its prey. "By the way, did Avastia show adverse effects to the liver?" Sonja snickered. "I saw those results in my preclinical studies too."

Sonja had the urge to kick Richard's cane out from under him, though she felt strangely thankful that he had stolen her discovery. She had realized in graduate school that Avastia would never work. It seemed that Richard had realized it as well, but by the time he had fully appreciated Avastia's harmful effects, it was too late to turn back. Not with hundreds of millions of dollars invested in Nautilus and countless patients waiting, hoping for a cure.

"I should be thanking you for stealing Avastia. I knew I would never be able to control the side effects. And neither could you. Yet you stole it and built a company around it. You built your whole career—whole *life*—on quicksand."

Hanging his head, Richard looked to be on the verge of tears. The knife was in his chest—Sonja intended to bury it deeper and twist.

"For years, I've waited for your world to crash down around you. A few months ago, that wish was granted. And to top it off, you received a cancer diagnosis."

"I'm taking Monty home with me."

"Impressive young man, Richard. It's a shame that Monty has so much of you in him. He cheated his way into my school because he didn't want to end up like dear ole dad. Noble, but misguided."

"I'm dying, Sonja. Let me take him home."

"No, Monty still has one final lesson left."

Monty watched Sonja charge through the doors of the conference hall where the dance was taking place. Recognizing the headmaster at the edge of the dance floor, the students stilled, and parents stopped their conversations. Sonja pointed to the DJ, who cut the music.

Mrs. Thompson rushed up to Sonja. "Dr. Woodward, it's so nice to see you again!"

Scanning the room, Sonja ignored her attempt at a handshake. "Thank you so much for helping Edwin." Mrs. Thompson glanced back at Edwin, who hadn't reacted to Sonja's arrival. He was eating a bowl of soup, one hand in his lap. "He's so much better now," Mrs. Thompson continued. "Calmer, kinder, so well-behaved."

Richard entered the room. Some parents gasped and whispered among themselves.

Mrs. Thompson stepped away from Sonja and turned to her husband. "Is that–"

Mr. Thompson nodded grimly.

Laura clutched Monty's arm. "Is that your dad?"

"Yeah," Monty whispered. It had only been three months, but his father's once-deep-brown hair had whitened since he last saw him. Breathing heavily, and with most of his weight pressed against his cane, it looked as if he might collapse at any moment.

Sonja pointed at Monty. "Montgomery Hughes!"

Hearing the last name "Hughes," there were murmurs

of confusion among Monty's classmates.

A narrow path parted on the dance floor, leading to Monty and Laura. Monty dropped his arm from Laura's side and stepped forward to face Sonja.

Richard passed Sonja and walked across the dance floor, stopping a few feet from Monty.

"Come with me, Monty."

"Who's he?" Jonathan asked, looking Richard up and down.

Richard coughed deeply into one hand, then stood up, straightening his back. "I'm Montgomery's father."

"I thought your last name was Hayward," Kirsten said.

Where could Monty possibly begin to explain the reason for his journey to Woodward? "Let me try to explain—"

"What does it matter?" Richard interrupted. "You don't belong here."

Monty glared at his father. "You're wrong."

"You faked your way here because of your dad?" Taylor asked, incredulous.

Monty's face flushed.

Richard signaled to Loretta that they were leaving and tried to grab Monty's arm.

Monty yanked his arm back, but he lost his footing and fell to the floor. He grunted as he smacked his elbow against the ground. When he looked up, Sonja was dangling a plastic bag between two fingers. Inside the bag were green buds that looked like marijuana. "We found this in your dorm room," Sonja said.

Monty knew that bag gave Sonja a reason to kick Monty out of the program, or worse. He thought about the prospect of receiving treatment. Wouldn't it ensure any possibility of future wrongdoing? Despite all of the readings and lessons, perhaps Monty needed it, after all? Maybe he had come to Woodward for it. Maybe treatment was his destiny.

"Mr. Aldrich, take Monty to Moralis, please."

Mr. Aldrich crossed the room like a bulldozer, shoving students aside.

Before he could reach Monty, though, Edwin stepped in front of him. "It's my bag!"

"What the hell are you doing, boy?" Mr. Thompson asked, grabbing Edwin's shoulder.

Edwin pushed his father away. "The right thing."

"Unfortunately, we have a zero-tolerance policy on substance abuse here at Woodward." Sonja turned to Mr. Aldrich. "Please show Edwin to his dorm room and allow him to collect his things. He and his parents can take the next ferry home."

Edwin's mouth fell open. "At least let me finish school with my friends."

"Dr. Woodward," Mrs. Thompson pleaded. "Please let him stay. He's different, can't you see? He's better. Woodward worked!"

Ignoring Edwin and his mother, Sonja widened her eyes at Mr. Aldrich.

Mr. Aldrich called two guards into the cluster of people. Each guard grabbed one of Edwin's arms, and they marched him toward the exit. The Thompsons followed behind, pleading for them to stop.

"As for Montgomery," Sonja said, turning to face Monty. "Assuming that Edwin's telling the truth and those drugs aren't yours, that doesn't excuse the fact that you've been lying to us all summer. And for that, there are consequences."

Mr. Aldrich grabbed the back of Monty's neck and yanked him toward the exit.

"Where are you taking him?" Richard yelled. He tried to follow, but a guard threw a hand across his chest, nearly toppling him over.

"It's time for Monty's final exam." Sonja looked at her watch and smiled at Richard. "I believe you are violating your house arrest, Dr. Hughes."

The doors to the conference hall burst open, and Holiday and a dozen FBI agents flooded the room. Richard reached for Monty weakly; the guard didn't have to work that hard to restrain him. A few inches from touching Monty, Richard slid a cell phone into one of Monty's jacket pockets, unnoticed.

Holiday pointed his pistol at Richard. "Hands above your head, Dr. Hughes!

Richard raised his hands and slowly lowered to his knees.

Holiday holstered his weapon and turned to Sonja. "We appreciate the tip, Dr. Woodward." He turned back to Richard. "It's time to go home, Dr. Hughes."

Sonja grinned as Mr. Aldrich pulled Monty off the dance floor, taking him to Moralis for treatment, and two FBI agents dragged Richard away, taking him home to his deathbed.

CHAPTER THIRTY-ONE

As the guards dragged Monty across the courtyard toward Moralis, a thunderstorm menaced Nantucket. The ocean was raging, the waves high and choppy. Monty lowered his head to protect his face from the pelting rain. Following behind him, Sonja tilted her umbrella sideways against the wind.

Monty knew that no one could protect him now. He would undergo treatment, and he would change, as Edwin had changed. He would become docile, obedient, no longer a threat to society or himself.

Monty heard a voice over the wind, calling from behind them. Turning his head as best he could in the guard's hold, he squinted through the rain to see Palmer sprinting across the courtyard, holding a hand up to shield his face.

Mr. Aldrich spun on his heels and lifted a palm, but Palmer blew past his warning.

"You can't do this, Sonja!" Palmer shouted.

Sonja followed the guards through the front doors of

Moralis and down the hallway. "It's obvious I'll have to perform the procedure tonight," she said without looking over her shoulder.

"He's not his father, Sonja!" Palmer said.

Sonja used her keycard to access the main lab and glanced back at Palmer. "I can't take that chance."

Dragging Monty into the lab, the guards slammed him into the treatment chair. Monty's chest heaved as they circled around him, securing his arms and legs with straps.

As Sonja went to the computer on one side of the room, Jessica pressed buttons on the CRISPR machine, and it hummed to life. She attached electrodes to Monty's chest and then moved to the corner of the room and prepared a sedative and a narcotic.

"Diphenhydramine?" Jessica asked.

"Twenty-five milligrams," Sonja said, clicking through files on a laptop.

Monty scanned Palmer's face for answers, for help, but he already knew his teacher was powerless.

"This technology goes too far," Palmer pleaded, standing in the doorway. "And we still don't know enough about how Edwin is reacting."

"What about Kirsten? Bet you're not worried about her." Sonja turned and grinned. "Oh, you thought I didn't know." She pointed to the surveillance cameras on the wall. "I know *everything* that happens here. Among the students *and* the faculty."

Jessica lowered Monty's chair into a semi-reclined position. Receiving a nod from Sonja, she administered the Benadryl. "Just a little prick," she warned Monty. Jessica slid the needle into a vein on his hand.

Biting her lip, Jessica lifted the syringe holding the

CRISPR solution and pressed on the plunger. When a little liquid squirted from the top, she looked at Sonja. "I'm not so sure this is a good idea, Dr. Woodward." Her voice was shaky. "Maybe we should listen to Dr. Reid?"

Sonja crossed the room and snatched the syringe from Jessica. Her eyes traveled back to Palmer. "You never understood the first thing about what I'm trying to do here, Palmer. These kids are a burden to society. Your burden. My burden. *Our* burden. We can stop crime before it starts. Think of the frauds we could prevent with this technology, the scams and scandals we could stop before they start. Think of the millions of dollars we'd spare from white-collar crime."

The drug was taking effect, and Monty began to feel lightheaded. Though his eyes had started to droop, he glanced at two cell phones lying on a nearby table—cell phones the guards had pulled from his pocket. *Two?* Monty thought he remembered feeling a tug on his jacket when his father had been close to him on the dance floor. He thought fast. "Before we do this, I want to call my father."

Sonja lowered the syringe.

"You're right, Dr. Woodward," Monty said. "I want to change."

Monty hoped he had sounded sincere. He just needed to get to the cell phone.

Sonja shook her head, set the syringe on the table, and grabbed a cell phone—

"No, the other one," Monty said.

Sonja grabbed the other phone and placed it in Monty's hand. A guard freed his hand so he could hold it. When he opened the phone, the screen displayed the name *David*

Holiday (FBI). Monty tilted the screen down, avoiding the gaze of the guard standing at his side. Tapping the screen, he dialed Holiday's number.

Can I tip him off? Get him to turn around and come to Moralis?

"This is Agent Holiday," answered a man's voice over the line.

"Dad, it's Monty." He thanked the drugs for keeping him from sounding too nervous.

Holiday sounded surprised. "How did you get this number?"

Monty was fighting a slur. "Dr. Woodward's about to deliver the treatment, and I just wanted to say that she's right: I'm a genetic mistake, and I'm supposed to be here."

There was silence on the other end of the line. *Has he caught on?*

Sonja laughed and began clapping. "Finally, he understands."

Monty subtly tilted the phone, so Holiday could hear Sonja's words.

"It's not an amoral act to fix your flawed genetic package," Sonja practically crooned. "Countless parents terminate pregnancies when prenatal tests show their children will have a developmental disorder or some imperfection that might make them less competitive in our fast-paced society. Why wouldn't the same be true when we identify genes that contribute to unethical behavior?"

"How many times do I have to tell you?" Palmer spoke up. "Our genes don't determine our destiny."

"Dr. Reid, the eternal idealist. The romantic. *Radical.*" Sonja shook her head.

"When are you going to see these kids for who they

really are? Damaged goods."

"Didn't you start Woodward because you knew a moral education could help prevent all this?" Palmer asked.

"We tried teaching—we tried the 'humane way'—but it doesn't work. Not for Edwin or Kirsten, and certainly not for Monty. And it won't work for any of these godforsaken teenagers. Do you really think philosophy can prevent another Richard Hughes?"

Palmer paced the room, looking stricken. "You never thought the classroom would work."

"Never had much faith in it, no. I always thought I'd have to rely on technology to get the job done."

"You've lost your mind, Sonja."

"Lost it?" She glared at Palmer. "I've never been more awake. You're the one who's asleep. The contents of this syringe give us the means to prevent our own downfall at the hands of con artists and psychopaths."

Monty leaned forward, hoping to better catch Sonja's rantings as she paced the floor. As he did, the drugs kicked in harder, making him sway. The phone slipped from his hand. He made a grab for it, but the drugs had him seeing double. The screen spiderwebbed as it hit the ground, but Monty could still see Holiday's name through the cracks.

As Monty watched, unable to move from the chair, Mr. Aldrich bent over, picked up the phone, and examined the screen.

"I think we have a problem, Dr. Woodward."

Taking the phone from Mr. Aldrich, Sonja stared at it, her eyes widening.

Palmer ran to Monty's side and pulled at one of the straps holding down his bound arm. In seconds, Mr.

Aldrich was on him, shoving him away. Palmer tumbled backward, knocking over a tray of instruments as he fell to the ground.

"Let me go!" Monty shouted, pulling at the second strap holding down his arm.

Sonja threw the phone to the ground, shattering it further, and stomped on it. Then she strode to a cabinet and pulled out a small silver pistol. Holding the gun in her hand, she spun around and approached Palmer, who had pushed himself up against one wall, his knees pressed to his chest.

Mt. Aldrich raised his hands cautiously. "Why do you have a gun, Dr. Woodward?"

"Let's just take a deep breath," the other guard added, inching toward her.

Sonja pointed the gun at Jessica. "Initiate the treatment!"

Jessica scanned Sonja's face, then Palmer's, looking unsure of what to do. Finally, she nodded and approached Monty, the syringe in her hand filled with the CRISPR package.

Sonja stood over Palmer with the gun pointed at his forehead. "Someone like you will never understand the measures that must be taken to protect society. You're weak. You'll never have the courage to do what I've done."

"You're playing God with these kids," Palmer said.

Sonja shoved the gun closer to Palmer's face. He closed his eyes, keeping his face pointed toward the gun. His body trembled with fear.

The room suddenly went black. Monty heard a burst of air behind him, indicating the main door had opened. "Lower your weapon, Dr. Woodward," a voice shouted.

Through the darkness, light and sound burst from the direction Monty had last seen Sonja. *Gunshots.* Two bursts answered from the door. The lights snapped on and Sonja was writhing on the floor, holding her stomach in agony.

Standing in the doorway, Holiday lowered his weapon as other FBI agents flooded into the room. An agent walked to Monty's side and removed the straps from his arms.

Holiday stepped closer, towering over the chair Monty had been strapped to. "Montgomery Hughes?"

Monty nodded.

"Thanks for calling." Holiday reached out and pulled Monty from the chair, still woozy from the drugs.

Another FBI agent called to Holiday from across the room. He walked over to find the agent hovering over Sonja. Monty joined him and watched as Sonja breathed shallowly.

"I did the right thing," Sonja said, her voice raspy. As blood oozed from her stomach, her eyes became glassy. She muttered something Monty couldn't understand, then her pupils fixed in place, and her body went limp.

Monty lowered down to one knee and stared at Sonja's lifeless body for a moment. It was then that all of Woodward's teachings clicked into place in his mind. Sonja had, in fact, believed she was doing the right thing. She had believed so strongly in the mission of Woodward, in the idea that she could help change—*protect*—humanity from wrongdoing, that she had blinded herself to the reality of her own morally dubious technology.

Monty stood up and turned to the agent. "Where's my father?"

"They're probably in Cape Cod by now," Holiday said.

"If I come home tonight, can I see him? There are some things I need to say before—"

"I'll make sure you have the privacy you need." Holiday clasped Monty's shoulder.

"But I'd hurry. I don't think he has much time."

CHAPTER THIRTY-TWO

An hour later, Monty zipped his duffel bag shut and scanned the dorm room. Three months ago, he had packed his belongings into the same bag, preparing for a summer at Woodward. Now he was returning home. How much had he changed? Had he gotten what he came to Woodward for? Had he vaccinated himself against future wrongs? He wasn't sure.

Leaving the dormitory, Monty crossed the courtyard. He still didn't know what to say to his father. Would he forgive him or disown him? Either way, he would die soon. A few hundred feet away, a horn blew loudly from the ferry as it prepared to leave for Cape Cod. Men on the docks were tossing ropes onto its deck. The ferry was leaving.

Monty ran down to the dock, but by the time he reached the end, the ferry was already ten feet away. People on the deck waved to him, but he lowered his head. "Shit."

A loud whistle cut through the air behind Monty.

"Going to Boston?"

Monty snapped his head up and around and found Wayne Price—the criminal turned speaker—standing at the wheel of a 40-foot-long V-shaped boat docked 50 feet away. Monty glanced at the departing ferry, then jogged toward the boat.

Wayne reached out and grabbed Monty's bag. "Jump in."

Monty hopped onto the boat. "What kind of boat is this?"

"I call it my go-fast boat." The engine roared to life, and Wayne revved it, producing a low gurgling sound.

At a table near the back sat a little boy.

"That's my son." Wayne nodded toward the boy. "Say hi, Mason."

The boy smiled and said hello.

Within minutes, the powerful boat had zoomed past the ferry and was skimming across the Atlantic Ocean at an unbelievable speed. The front of the boat bobbed as it cut through choppy waves.

"How fast are we going?" Monty yelled over the engine.

"Eighty miles per hour."

"How long until we get to the Cape?"

"About an hour and forty-five minutes."

Monty noticed Wayne's son fiddling with an oxygen tank. The boy pressed a button on the tank, and air hissed.

"Don't play with that, Mason."

Ignoring his father, the boy turned the nozzle again to create another hiss. Then he started shuffling through other equipment in a nearby compartment.

Wayne sighed. "I was inside when he was born," he

told Monty. "He was eight when we first met. I'm trying to get to know him." He laughed. "He's trying to keep me a stranger."

As he listened, Monty watched the ocean. The water was calm, the opposite of how he was feeling—tense, anxious, conflicted. An image of Sonja's locked eyes flashed into his mind and he tried to shake away the image. Her last words still rang in his ears:

"I did the right thing."

"I wasn't a bad family man," Wayne continued. "I just had one set of values at home and another at work. I screwed up, but I love that little guy more than anything."

As the boat sped toward the cape, Monty took a seat and struggled with what he wanted to say to his dad. Would he tell him that he wasn't the man he thought he was? Would he apologize for leaving without telling him? Would he forgive him for what he did? *Could* he?

When Monty arrived home, Holiday greeted him at the door. As Monty rolled his wheeled duffel bag through the mudroom, his eyes landed on a stack of envelopes on the dining room table. Many had been opened and papers lay strewn across the table.

"Letters from all over the country, addressed to your father." Holiday shook his head. "Not exactly fan mail."

Setting down his bag, Monty picked up a letter and began reading. It was from a mother whose son had died after a month of being on Avastia. She wrote that Richard had given them false hope. She blamed Richard for her son's death.

Monty read another letter. It was filled with hate.

Monty walked past the spare bedroom and saw his mother was lying on the bed. Her eyes were closed, dark circles spreading around them. She was taking a nap—resting her eyes, as she called it. He hadn't realized it then, but he should have told her where he was going three months ago. His chest tightened with guilt.

Monty knelt beside her and clasped her hand. Her eyes slit open, then flew wide.

"Monty!" She threw her arms around him. "I've missed you so much."

Monty hugged her tight. "I missed you too, Mom."

She rose quickly, her expression nervous, and rushed across the living room to the kitchen. "Are you hungry?" Monty didn't have time to answer before he was following her, watching as she busily opened the refrigerator and pulled plates from cabinets.

Monty stood on the other side of the kitchen island. "Why didn't you tell me about his fraud?"

Elizabeth closed the cabinet slowly. Her hand still on the handle, she lowered her head. "Let me make you a grilled cheese sandwich," she whispered. "You used to love those when you were young."

She hadn't made him a grilled cheese sandwich in years. "I'm not that hungry."

"Remember how I used to cut the crust off your sandwiches?" Her eyes filled with tears, but she opened the refrigerator and searched inside. Her hands shook as she pulled out butter, cheese, and bread and spread the items out onto the counter. She sprayed a frying pan with oil. "Anyone who cuts the crust from a sandwich really cares."

"Mom."

The tears began streaming down her face. "I wanted to tell you, but I knew it would crush you. I know how high a regard you hold him in." She wiped her eyes and glanced at Monty. "How high a regard you *used* to hold him in." She used a knife to butter a slice of bread, which she then placed in the pan. She put a slice of cheese on top of it and another slice of bread atop that.

"Your father is a complex man, Monty," she said.

"Do you love him?"

"Of course, I love your father. He swept me away. And I had no reason to question his research. No one questioned him—certainly not me."

Monty sighed. "You know, I have these scattered images of him from my childhood. This summer, I would run through some of them, and I realized that his fraud was always there inside him, waiting to emerge. It was in his DNA, you could say. His fraud—his crime—was his destiny. His character was his destiny."

Silently, she set the grilled cheese sandwich on the counter in front of Monty.

Monty picked at the sandwich. "What I still don't get is how the FBI knew. Someone must have—"

He snapped his gaze up and stared at his mother. She wouldn't meet his eyes.

"We built a life together. I watched him rise to great heights. I stood by him through everything. But what he did—did you see those letters? It was unforgivable." She sobbed. "But I'm so ashamed for turning him in. It's unbearable. I just want to sleep and never wake up."

"Someone had to do something, Mom. It took courage to tell someone. At the time, I didn't have the courage. I'm proud of you."

Elizabeth nodded. "He's dying. He'll go to jail, but the family will carry his shame."

"No, Mom." Monty bit into the sandwich and stood up. "The shame dies with him tonight." He put the sandwich down and left the kitchen to find his father.

Crossing the dining room, Monty found Holiday sitting at the long mahogany table. He sat alone, staring into a cup of coffee.

"I cleared the room, Monty. No agents. It'll just be you and him."

"How is he?" Monty asked.

"The nurse left for the night. She said he's going downhill. His kidneys and liver are failing. She was giving him intravenous adrenaline to keep his blood pressure up, but she stopped, so it's only a matter of time now."

"Thank you." Monty continued across the dining room.

As he entered the living room, he heard the faint beep of a heart monitor. Then he saw his father, slumped in a wheelchair, breathing sluggishly.

Richard seemed to notice Monty at about the same time. He raised his hand weakly. His sweatshirt was too large for his emaciated body, and his eyes were sunken, surrounded by dark wrinkles. Monty wondered how this dying man had escaped his house arrest and made it to Nantucket to confront Sonja and him.

Richard tried to say something—"You're home," perhaps—but the words were jumbled, and Monty couldn't understand them.

Monty sat in a chair and rolled it toward Richard's wheelchair. He placed his elbows on his knees and looked his father in the eye. He took a deep breath. "You kept a lie going for so long."

Richard unlocked his wheelchair and inched it closer to Monty. His words were still hard to understand. "The whole thing got away from me."

Monty shook his head. "You failed, Dad. And you just couldn't accept it."

"I hope that you never get put in a situation like I—"

Richard broke into a coughing fit and turned his head as it took its course. When it stopped, he turned back.

"A situation where you could cross the line."

"Do you feel sorry for what you did?"

"I feel relief, Monty. I'm relieved that it's almost over."

Monty turned and scanned the family pictures on the hearth—warm memories of summers on Nantucket.

Richard closed his eyes and his breathing gave way to another cough. "We gave you the best life. We raised you with good values. Why did you think you needed to go to Woodward?"

Monty's mind drifted back to that day he had shadowed his father in the hospital. So exhausted, Richard had given a patient the wrong medication. He had made a mistake. Did he tell someone? Fill out a safety report? The patient was fine, so "no harm, no foul." That was how his father worked within the gray areas of his life.

"I used to spend every waking moment trying to prove that I was enough to you. I realized there would be no end to that. No happiness there."

"I loved you the only way I knew how."

Monty shook his head.

Richard looked at the hospital bed and then studied the floor. "Help me into my bed, Monty."

Monty looked at his father—*really* looked. For the first time in years, Richard seemed content. The confession seemed to have lifted a weight from him. Monty thought about the journaling he had done over the summer. His conversations with Palmer. All the readings. Monty loved his father, but he realized that he had already lost him years ago. He'd lost his father as the man became so focused on building Nautilus that he had little time for fatherhood. Monty was grieving the loss of his father long before this night.

Monty stood and slid his arms underneath his father's. He wrapped his arms around his father, squeezing the man's chest to his own, and lifted him from his seat. Richard groaned his way to a standing position, wobbled, and fell into Monty's arms. Monty hugged him tightly to stabilize him. The motion was surprisingly comforting, and Monty realized suddenly that he hadn't touched his father in years. His father hadn't even been this close to him since Monty was a toddler. Moisture clouded Monty's vision, and he began to cry softly.

Sniffling, Monty laid Richard down in his bed, making sure that the tubes and wires stayed connected and didn't tangle. He placed a pillow under his father's head.

Richard gripped Monty's hand. "I don't have time, but you have your whole life ahead of you. It's a great life, I know it. And maybe you can make things right. We had a good name once. Get it back."

Monty leaned over and stroked his father's hair. "It's all right," he said. "I want you to know that it's all right."

"You were always good, Monty," Richard said, his

voice beginning to drift. “The best man I know.”

Monty covered his father’s hand with one of his own. Richard’s eyes closed, and his breathing slowed. For the first time, Monty knew that he wasn’t going to travel the same path as his father. Sitting in silence, he realized that he had become his own man, the best one he was capable of being.

Too soon, his father’s chest stopped moving, and his breath gave out.

CHAPTER THIRTY-THREE

Several days later, Woodward Academy had become a crime scene. FBI agents and other authorities roamed the halls, passing in and out of the main building, carrying equipment and files, and interviewing faculty and staff. Through a window in Palmer's classroom, Monty watched a policeman unraveling caution tape near the fountain in the courtyard.

"Are we allowed to be here?" Jonathan asked.

Palmer was sitting on top of his desk at the front of the classroom. "The FBI has evacuated Woodward and Moralis, but Agent Holiday knows we are here. I know most of your parents are waiting for you at the ferry landing, so this shouldn't take long. I just thought we should all meet before you left to go home."

"Do we get like a diploma, or something?" Cory asked.

"My dad graduated from anger management and even he got a certificate," Jonathan said.

"There won't be any graduation ceremony, or diplomas," Palmer said.

"What will you do now, Dr. Reid?" Monty asked. "Will you go back to Boston?"

Palmer shook his head. "I'll be sticking around here, see if I can make some changes. Dr. Woodward's work wasn't entirely flawed." He pointed to a stack of papers on his desk. "I finished her congressional report, citing all the flaws and blatant disregard for regulations."

"What's the first order of business?" Edwin asked.

"Obviously, Moralis's bio-enhancement program has been shut down," Palmer said. "I want to hire more mental health experts—psychologists and social workers—so we can offer interventions to treat adverse childhood experiences. Not every human problem can be solved with technology."

"Sometimes it takes a human to solve a very human problem," Monty replied.

Palmer smiled.

"So, are we still 'bad apples'?" Taylor asked.

"Do you feel any different?" Palmer asked.

"If a boss asks me to do something questionable someday," Taylor said, "I feel like I'll think twice."

Monty thought about the question. At the start of the summer, they had been labeled the 'bad ones'—destined, it seemed, to skirt rules, cheat systems, and maybe even break laws. Had they neutralized their genetic predispositions? Time would tell.

"Remember that a flourishing life—a happy life—is a virtuous one, and that the path to virtue is not to study what it means to be virtuous, but to live virtue. And that's my final lesson to you, graduating students: Don't tell me you are living a virtuous life. *Show* me."

Palmer ended the class, and one by one, the students

walked to the front of the classroom and shook his hand. When it was his turn, Edwin turned in his seat toward Monty and, with a sarcastic grin, punched him in the arm playfully. Palmer shook Edwin's hand proudly.

Palmer motioned for Monty to come to the front. After shaking hands with his teacher, the two hugged. "Thank you, Dr. Reid," Monty said, "For everything."

"I'm proud of you." Palmer patted Monty on the back before letting him go.

"Congrats, roomie," Edwin said.

"You too, man." Monty shook Edwin's hand and squinted. "How are you . . . feeling?"

Edwin ran a hand through his hair and shook his head. "Well, last night, Dr. Reid brought me into the lab. These scientists said they had found a way to turn off the genes Sonja's technology had turned on. These empathy genes, I guess."

"So, you're back to normal?" Monty asked, surprised. "Whatever *normal* is?"

"I told them not to reverse it." Edwin grinned. "What's so wrong with feeling everything?"

Monty laughed, appreciating the sentiment. If his empathy didn't overwhelm Edwin and handicap him, perhaps being overly empathetic wasn't such a bad thing. Such a disorder—if it could be called that—might even be a benefit.

"Oh, hey! Check this out!" Edwin pulled out his phone, opened the web browser, and turned his phone so Monty could see the article on the screen. It was a news story co-written by Edwin and Amy Baker: "Headmaster of Woodward Dead: What Will Become of The Empathy Academy?"

Monty grinned. "You finally got that big story you wanted."

"He's got a fine career ahead of him." Palmer was grinning at Edwin. "Just as long as he plays by the rules from now on."

"And you?" Edwin asked. "What does the future hold for Mr. *Hughes*?"

"Hopefully it will be *Doctor* Hughes someday."

"Walking in your father's footsteps after all?"

Monty nodded. "His steps, *not* his missteps."

After saying his goodbye, Monty walked across the courtyard and saw Laura standing on the dock, where Monty had docked his father's 30-foot sailboat, which he had sailed from the Cape the day before.

Laura pulled a newspaper clipping from her pocket and handed it to Monty. It was a poem from the arts and culture section of Nantucket's newspaper. "I got my first poem published."

"Congratulations, Laura."

Laura grinned. "Call me when you get to Boston."

"I will." Monty smiled and kissed Laura softly. "See you soon."

Laura backed up and, one by one, Monty threw off the dock lines and prepared the boat for sea. As the boat made its way out of the harbor, Monty looked back at Nantucket Island—a rock in the Atlantic that had seemed so far away, so isolated when the summer began. He pictured the island as it had looked that first day. The dark ocean, the gray clouds overhead, and the thin rain that had stung his face. This evening, the deep blue ocean water was calm, there wasn't a cloud in the sky, and an orange sun hung over the horizon.

Monty thought about empathy—the capacity to put himself in someone else's shoes, to see through their eyes, to feel their pain—and how society wouldn't be possible without it. He still didn't know if empathy could be taught but having spent the summer at Woodward, he felt better prepared to face the moral complexities that would no doubt come his way in life. Hopefully, he'd be able to avoid the failings he'd witnessed in the people closest to him.

Monty had learned much from Palmer's teachings and the shortcomings of Edwin and Wayne, from the moral weaknesses of Sonja and his father who's actions had set his journey in motion. Having forgiven Richard before the cancer took his life, Monty no longer carried the weight of his father's shame. He felt lighter and freer to become the man he knew he could be. Still, Monty had a long life ahead of him. College, medical school, a future career in medicine. There would be moral and ethical challenges through all of it.

Of course, Monty wouldn't know how much he'd learned until he was presented with his own moral challenges. Would he stand up to petty, small people when others remained quiet? Would he speak truth to power when doing so might be dangerous? Would he look the other way in the face of tyranny?

Monty hoped he'd have the guts to stand up and intervene if something wasn't right. But doing the right thing would take courage—a trait Monty knew he had. He hadn't inherited courage, he'd developed it. And that courage would help him lead a virtuous life, the only life truly worth living, he'd realized.

As the sailboat moved away from the island, the wind whipped Monty's hair back and forth. In the distance, a blue whale broke the water's surface and sprayed water high into the air. A firm grip on the wheel, Monty steadied the boat and pointed it toward home.

ACKNOWLEDGEMENTS

Thank you to everyone who discussed this book with me and helped improve it through thoughtful conversation. I owe a debt of gratitude to teachers and students of the Solstice MFA Program, where I wrote and revised most of this novel. Thank you to Solstice faculty members David Yoo, Sandra Scofield, and Venise Berry for their insights on the craft of writing and for improving this story in countless ways. Thanks also to Solstice students Al Leftwich, Mark Jednaszewski, and Martin Smith for workshopping early pages.

I'd also like to thank my editor, Tod Tinker, for his impeccable line-editing and fact-checking skills as well as for revealing flaws in my logic or thinking. Thanks to the talented team at Atmosphere Press for believing in this book and making it a reality. A special thank you to Sam Cooke for always listening to my ideas, reading my work, and stoking the fires of my passion for writing and storytelling.

ABOUT ATMOSPHERE PRESS

Atmosphere Press is an independent, full-service publisher for excellent books in all genres and for all audiences. Learn more about what we do at atmospherepress.com.

We encourage you to check out some of Atmosphere's latest releases, which are available at Amazon.com and via order from your local bookstore:

Twisted Silver Spoons, a novel by Karen M. Wicks
Queen of Crows, a novel by S.L. Wilton
The Summer Festival is Murder, a novel by Jill M. Lyon
The Past We Step Into, stories by Richard Scharine
The Museum of an Extinct Race, a novel by Jonathan Hale Rosen
Swimming with the Angels, a novel by Colin Kersey
Island of Dead Gods, a novel by Verena Mahlow
Cloakers, a novel by Alexandra Lapointe
Twins Daze, a novel by Jerry Petersen
Embargo on Hope, a novel by Justin Doyle
Abaddon Illusion, a novel by Lindsey Bakken
Blackland: A Utopian Novel, by Richard A. Jones
The Jesus Nut, a novel by John Prather
The Embers of Tradition, a novel by Chukwudum Okeke
Saints and Martyrs: A Novel, by Aaron Roe

ABOUT THE AUTHOR

DUSTIN GRINNELL is the author of *The Genius Dilemma* and *Without Limits*. His work has appeared in *The Boston Globe*, *The Washington Post*, *New Scientist*, *Salon*, *VICE*, and *Writer's Digest*, among many other popular and literary publications. He earned his MFA in fiction from the Solstice MFA Program, and his MS in physiology from Penn State. He grew up in the White Mountains of New Hampshire and now lives in Boston, Massachusetts.

www.dustingrinnell.com

CPSIA information can be obtained
at www.ICGtesting.com
Printed in the USA
LVHW041644270122
709553LV00008B/735